# THE SAVAGE TRAP

## THE UNPRODUCED SCREENPLAY

### IB MELCHIOR

Published in the USA by:
BearManor Media
PO Box 1129
Duncan, Oklahoma 73534-1129
*www.bearmanormedia.com*

ISBN 978-1-59393-392-0

Printed in the United States of America.
Book design by Brian Pearce | Red Jacket Press.

# INTRODUCTION

On of the most strategically located — and for the security of the USA, tactically, vitally important safeguards — is the Panama Canal. What better location for a rip-roaring, action escapade with international implications, I thought, than this unique area — and *The Savage Trap* was set. The screenplay was written in early 1958, the second script written for the prominent Philadelphia surgeon, Victor P. Satinsky, whose ambitious avocation was movie making, and who wanted an action story. The first had been *The Micro Men*, which for reasons remained unproduced. Satinsky finally abandoned this project, as well. I assume he ran into the same problems I did, later on.

The Canal, at that time, was owned by the United States, which bought it in 1904 and built it into a vital international waterway — but at the time of writing the screenplay, rumblings for a change in the US Government were already rampant. I thought this state of affairs would be a hot, topical, up-to-date subject for a really unusual action feature-length motion picture. I was wrong. Rather than generating interest in the canal, the disturbing discussions of a "change" left potential producers with a hands-off attitude.

The main action of the script I wrote takes place in the wild jungle between the Canal Zone and Columbia, where the native Indian tribes were still quite uncivilized. The story takes advantage of their native cunning — displayed in their sometimes violent intertribal conflicts — with various ingenious, deadly and sometimes gruesome traps, modeled after actual such contraptions. Events spill over into Washington, D.C., and the Pentagon.

Producers and studios unanimously found the script fascinating — but because of the unpredictable political ramifications, they left the screenplay to wither on a Hollywood vine, and it gradually became obsolete in its premise. The death knell came when in 1979 President Jimmy Carter simply gave the US rights to the Canal away. The result was that China bought the Canal, and is today the owner. The crucial waterway, which once served as a safety shield at the vulnerable soft underbelly of the United States, is today owned and controlled by the Chinese. I mention this because, coincidentally, the screenplay of *The Savage Trap* definitely identifies the mysterious invader as "an oriental power." Fiction becomes fact…

*Ib Melchior*

# T H E   S A V A G E   T R A P

by
Ib Melchior

**The Coppage Company**
3369 Canton Lane
Studio City, CA 91604
(818) 980-8806

# T H E   S A V A G E   T R A P

## C A S T

| | | | |
|---|---|---|---|
| STEVEN CARTER | 36 | American | Male Lead |
| NENITA ARIAS | 22 | Panamanian | Female Lead |
| COL. SHIPLEY BANKES, U.S.A.F. | 45 | American | Feature |
| ALAN GRANT, C.I.A. AGENT | 33 | American | Feature |
| COL. GREGOR STEPAN | 40 | European | Feature |
| SAGALA COMAN | 35 | Indian | Feature |
| TOM WARNECKE, C.I.A. AGENT | 28 | American | |
| EMILIO MANUEL ARIAS | 5? | Panamanian | |
| ENEEPE | 16 | Indian | |
| DIETRICH | 36 | European | |
| VARNOFF | 38 | European | |
| ZABALA | 35 | Panamanian | |
| JANET HUNTER | 24 | American | |
| DONALD HARRISON | 54 | American | |
| FRANK DUNCAN, C.I.A. | 50 | American | |

## B I T S   &   E X T R A S

| | | |
|---|---|---|
| CARLOS MENDEZ | 42 | Panamanian |
| HUNTED CONTOOLIE | 32 | Indian |
| SERGEANT, U.S.A.F. | 25 | American |
| MAJ. ROBERT S. WARD, U.S.A.F. | 38 | American |
| TERUI | 34 | Indian |
| MOON FEAST MAID | 14 | Indian |
| C.I.A. AGENT | 30 | American |
| DIEGO | 27 | Indian/Panamanian |
| JOSE | 26 | Indian/Panamanian |
| LT. JUAN HERRARA, PANAMANIAN POLICE FORCE | 29 | Panamanian |
| VILLAGER | 45 | Panamanian |

Bar Customers, U.S. Armed Personnel, Indians and Panamanian Villagers, 3 Cargadores, Stepan's men, General Atmosphere.

\* \* \* \* \* \*

NOTE: THE SCRIPT RUNS LONG IN PAGE COUNT BECAUSE IT IS BROKEN DOWN INTO INDIVIDUAL SHOTS. IT IS, HOWEVER, DESIGNED AS A LOW BUDGET, 90 to 100 MINUTE MOTION PICTURE TO BE FILMED IN SOUTH AMERICA OR MEXICO.

# THE SAVAGE TRAP

Original Screenplay
by
Ib Melchior

BEFORE MAIN TITLE AND CREDITS

FADE IN

1. EXT. DAY. MED. L.S. JUNGLE

It is a wild, tropical jungle; the vegetation is richly
green and luxuriant; in the F.G. is a small clearing;
the whole place has a primeval, untamed look about it;
there is a deathly hush of menacing anticipation in the
air...

Suddenly there is a small noise - and a man breaks through
the jungle growth across the clearing to stand for a
moment at the edge of the jungle; it is an Indian; his
scant clothing is ripped and torn; around his neck he
wears a leather string with half a dozen unidentifiable
objects hanging from it; he staggers slightly; he is
obviously exhausted - and terrorized...

He listens for a brief moment; faintly in the ominous
silence the sounds of pursuit can be heard coming from
behind him; desperately he begins to run across the
clearing, towards camera...

He reaches a MED. CLOSE UP; his face is wild with panic
and fear; he breathes quick gulps of air; he is near
collapse...

All at once there is the shock report of a high powered
rifle; the Indian staggers as if from a sharp blow; his
hand flies to his right shoulder; his face writhes in the
tortured grimace of pain and dread; his mouth opens in a
silent scream - and he starts to spin around from the
force of the bullet impact...

2. ANOTHER ANGLE. MED. SHOT

The Indian spins half way around; he starts to sink to
the ground; there is another shot - and another; the
bullets whizz by the terror-stricken man; with a tremendous effort he catches himself - and half staggers,
half runs into the jungle...

3. MED. SHOT. JUNGLE SWAMP

The Indian comes lurching through the jungle; he is
barely able to keep on his feet; he comes to a small
swamp pool; exhausted he lowers himself into the slimy,
murky water - and hides himself by pulling weeds and
grass over his head; the sounds of several men running

3. CONTINUED:                                                    2.

   through the jungle in swift pursuit can be heard -
   coming ever closer...

4. C. U. INDIAN

   His eyes bulge wide with fear; he is trying not to
   breathe too loudly; the noise of running men comes
   closer...

5. SHOT. INDIAN'S P.O.V.

   Through the weeds and grass the swampland can be made
   out; the pursuers are almost upon the hiding place...

   Suddenly a pair of legs, and only the legs, can be seen -
   and heard - splashing through the mud; clad in gray
   trousers they wear heavy, high, black boots!

6. CLOSE SHOT. INDIAN

   He shrinks back as far as he can into his hiding place,
   suddenly there is a faint, hissing sound behind him;
   he turns his head to look - and almost screams in
   shocked fright...

7. MED. CLOSE SHOT. INDIAN AND BRUSH BEHIND HIM

   In the thick brush on the bank behind the cowering man
   a huge python snake is slowly slithering towards the
   petrified Indian - closer and closer...

   The man frantically tries to draw away from the menacing, coldly staring reptile - and still remain hidden
   from the booted pursuers splashing by only a few feet
   away!

8. ANGLE. INDIAN AND PYTHON

   The snake is within striking distance; the last pair of
   booted legs can be seen splashing by - and quickly
   disappearing in the distance...

   And suddenly - without warning - the huge python strikes
   straight for the Indian's arm, raised in a desperate
   attempt to ward off the deadly attack...

   As the snake strikes - the Main Title jumps in super-
   imposed over the scene:

                    T H E  S A V A G E  T R A P

   Camera pans off the struggling man along the python's

3.

8.   CONTINUED:

body; as the whole length of the snake slowly glides
from the brush into the swamp, the Credits follow the
main title in superimposition over the scene, until
camera holds on empty brush; the splashing, panting,
hissing and tearing of the mighty battle can be
heard throughout; occasionally the brush shakes
violently...

As the last credit fades out - so does the sound of
the fight....

                              DISSOLVE

9.   STOCK.
     CAPITOL BUILDING, WASHINGTON, D.C., DAY.

10.  STOCK.
     PENTAGON BUILDING, WASHINGTON, D.C., DAY.

11.  INT. DAY.  OFFICE OF COL. SHIPLEY BANKES, USAF. MED. SHOT

The office is functionally furnished; on one wall is a
large map of Panama with the Canal Zone featured; another
map showing the entire world with shipping routes marked
to indicate the canal traffic, occupies another wall;
the office is that of an Air Force officer; behind a
desk sits a uniformed man in his late forties; a name
plate on the desk identifies his as Col. Shipley Bankes,
U.S.A.F.; he is talking on the telephone; he is obviously quite excited, though trying not to show it.

Camera dollies in to a MED. C.U., during:

                    BANKES
                  (on phone)
          Of course, Dr. Ambrose... I under-
          stand...And as far as you know, he
          is the only one?...I see...Yes, I
           have it:  Columbia University,
          New York...Thank you for your
          cooperation, Doctor...and please
          remember:  Keep this in the
          strictest confidence...Right!...
          Good-bye!...

He hangs up - and shouts.

                    BANKES
          Ser-geant!

12. ANOTHER ANGLE

The door opens almost at once, and the Sergeant enters.

                    SERGEANT
          Sir?

Col. Bankes gets up from his·deask; he puts some papers
and documents in a briefcase, and shrugs into his blouse,
during:

                    BANKES
          Get me a car at once...I am going
          to the C.I.A. Building...

                    SERGEANT
          Yes, Sir...

                    BANKES
          And order a jet flight to stand
          by - for an immediate flight to
          New York!

                    SERGEANT
          Yes, Sir!

He turns and walks out quickly; Bankes is ready; he picks
up his cap and starts to walk out; on the way he passes
the Panama wall map; he pauses to glance at it; he frowns;
then - resolutely - he walks off.

Camera holds on the map, and slowly dollies in...

                    DISSOLVE

13. AERIAL SHOT.  DAY.  NEW YORK SKYLINE (STOCK)

14. AERIAL SHOT.  DAY  STATUE OF LIBERTY. (STOCK)

15. ESTABLISHING SHOT.  EMPIRE STATE BUILDING.  DAY

16. ESTABLISHING SHOT.  UNITED NATIONS BUILDING.  DAY

17. L.S.  DAY.  COLUMBIA UNIVERSITY MAIN BUILDING

18. CLOSE SHOT.  LEGEND OVER MAIN ENTRANCE.

The legend establishes the building as Columbia University.

19. L.S.  DAY.  MAIN ENTRANCE OF COLUMBIA UNIVERSITY.

Two men (one of them is Alan Grant - or double -, a big

man in his thirties) come down the steps hurriedly and
enter a car, which takes off fast...

                              DISSOLVE

20. L.S. DAY. BROWNSTONE HOUSE. WASHINGTON SQUARE AREA, N.Y.

The car is parked in front of the house; the two men are
talking with the building superintendent standing on the
steps; he shakes his head; the two men quickly go to the
car...

                              DISSOLVE

21. L.S. DAY. TAXI GARAGE.

Several Taxis are in evidence; there is general activity
as the cars leave and arrive at the garage parking area;
the two men are standing talking to a dispatcher;  then
they walk to their own car...

                              DISSOLVE

22. L.S. NIGHT. ROCKEFELLER CENTER

The impressive buildings are all lit up.

23. L.S. NIGHT. TIMES SQUARE

The multitude of neon signs are flashing their gaudy
lights.

24. INT. NIGHTCLUB BAR. MED. SHOT

The bar is well attended; among the customers is a couple
of young people; a stunning blonde escorted by a handsome, well built young man; it is Steve Carter; he is
likable, about 26 years of age, intelligent; soft piano
music is playing in the background...

Camera dollies in to a TWO SHOT.

The two young people are engaged in a serious conversa-
tion.

                         STEVE
                       (soberly)
            I'm sorry, Janet, really I am...
            But I can't make a decision just
            like that...

> JANET
> (Displeased)
Oh, Steve! Why don't you wake
up!

> STEVE
I'm a scientist, Jan, not a
business man...

> JANET
> (pouting)
You won't even try...

> STEVE
Look, Jan, my interest - my
work - is anthropology...the
study of mankind...

> JANET
> (Heatedly)
What earthly good is it to know
about a lot of silly aborigines?
> (suddenly seductive)
With Dad you could make real good
money...You'll never make anything
puttering around those musty museums
of yours...

> STEVE
Janet...

> JANET
...And playing hostess to a lot
of old fossils when we get married
certainly isn't my idea of fun...
If you'd only go in with Dad - it'd
be so much better...

> STEVE
> (Trying to make light of
> a situation that is threat-
> ening to become difficult)
I'd make a very poor v.p., Jan...
besides, I don't have a middle
initial...Every self respecting
vice president has a middle initial!

25. WIDER ANGLE

Through the crowd two men can be seen purposefully making their way toward Steve and Janet at the bar; it is
the two men we have seen before; one of them is Alan
Grant.

25. CONTINUED

Janet deliberately takes off her engagement ring and
places it on the bar.

                        JANET
                       (Cooly)
          When you reconsider - so will I!
          Goodbye, Stevie!...

Gets up to leave.

                        STEVE
                     (Seriously)
          Janet, listen to me...

But she walks off; Steve almost follows her, but thinks
better of it; he picks up the ring, and hails the bar-
tender.

                        STEVE
          Give me a double Scotch...Make it
          a tripple!...

The two men have reached Steve; Grant taps him on the
shoulder; Steve turns to him.

                        GRANT
          Mr. Carter?  Mr. Steven Carter?...

                        STEVE
                      (Puzzled)
          Yes?...

Grant holds out an I.D. card for Steve to see.

                        GRANT
          We had quite a time tracking you
          down...

26. TWO SHOT.  STEVE AND GRANT

Steve looks at the I.D. card; he reacts.

                        GRANT
                      (Quietly)
          I'm Alan Grant - Central Intelligence
          Agency...We must ask you to come with
          us, Mr. Carter.

                        STEVE
                     (Startled)
          Why?  What's the matter?

                        GRANT
          All I can tell you now is - you are

                                        (cont.)

>                    GRANT
>                    (Cont.)
> wanted in Washington on a most
> urgent matter...
>
>                    STEVE
>                    (Astonished)
> Washington?!
>
>                    GRANT
> There's an Air Force jet waiting to
> take you there...
>
>                    STEVE
> Is this a joke?...
>
>                    GRANT
> I assure you it is not...
>
>                    STEVE
> But - I can't just leave like that!
> I have classes to teach - at the
> University - tomorrow...
>
>                    GRANT
> We've already cleared that with
> the Dean
>
>                    STEVE
>                    (Startled)
> You have?!  Well...If it's that
> important...You can wait one hour,
> can't you?...
>
>                    GRANT
>                    (Firmly)
> We can, Mr. Carter.  Washington can't!

Steve looks at the man searchingly; Grant looks grim
and determined; with a small puzzled frown Steve shrugs
his shoulders.

27.  WIDER ANGLE

They start to walk off...

>                                        DISSOLVE

28.  EXT. NIGHT. L.S. NATIONAL AIRPORT, WASHINGTON, D.C.
     (STOCK)

An Air Force Jet plane is landing.

>                                        CUT TO:

29.   EXT. NIGHT. L.S. FRONT ENTRANCE OF WALTER REED HOSPITAL
      IN WASHINGTON, D.C.

      A car drives up in front of the Hospital; two men (Steve
      and Grant) get out and hurry into the building.

30.   CLOSE SHOT. SIGN ON BUILDING IDENTIFYING IT AS THE
      WALTER REED HOSPITAL.

31.   INT. HOSPITAL CORRIDOR.  MED. L.S.

      In the F. G. two Air Force M.P.'s stand guard at a door;
      in the B. G. Steve and Grant round a corner and walk up
      to the guards, who stop them; Grant shows his I.D. card.

                    GRANT
                (To the guards)
          This is Mr. Steven Carter.
                (To Steve)
          Please wait here.

      They stand aside to let Grant enter the room; he does -
      reappearing almost at once.

                    GRANT
          Please come in, Mr. Carter.

      He holds the door open for Steve; Steve starts to enter..

32.   INT. HOSPITAL ROOM.  WIDE ANGLE SHOT

      It is a typical, large hospital room; the bed is hidden
      by a screen; there are four people present; Col. Bankes,
      who is in earnest conversation with a small, dark civi-
      lian, Carlos Mendez; another man in civilian clothes,
      about fifty years of age, is standing near the window
      smoking a pipe; a doctor is busy at a small instrument
      table; presently he goes behind the screen with a syringe..

      Steve enters the room; Grant follows him and closes the
      door behind him remaining standing at the door; Col.
      Bankes at once turns to Steve.

                    BANKES
          Mr. Carter...Thank you for coming...
          I'm Col. Shipley Bankes...

                   STEVE
          How are you, Colonel...

      Bankes looks at him with a penetrating look.

                    BANKES
          Mr. Carter.  Whatever you learn here
          tonight is classified 'top secret'!...
          Is that clear?

                    STEVE
          I understand.

                    BANKES
          Good.
               (He turns to Mendez)
          I want you to meet Mr. Carlos Mendez
          of the Panamanian Embassy.

     Steve and Mendez exchange greetings; Bankes turns to
     the man at the window.

                    BANKES
          And this is Mr. Donald Harrison...

33.  C. U.  STEVE

     He turns and sees Harrison for the first time; he reacts
     with astonishment; he is impressed.

                    STEVE
          Mr. Harrison...

34.  GROUP SHOT

     Harrison walks over to Steve; he has an air of great
     authority and calm about him.

                    HARRISON
          Nice to meet you, Mr. Carter...
          I'm told you may be able to help
          us...

                    BANKES
               (To Steve)
          I must ask you to forget that you
          saw Mr. Harrison here tonight!

                    STEVE
               (puzzled)
          Oh - alright!!...

                    HARRISON
               (With a little smile)
          The White House's interest in this
          matter, Mr. Carter, is - as yet -
          unofficial!...

                    STEVE
          What can I do, sir?

                    BANKES
          Dr. Ambrose of the Smithsonian
          Institution here in Washington
          informed us that you are an
          anthropologist on the staff of
          Columbia University in New York...
          Is that correct?

                    STEVE
          It is.

                    BANKES
          He also told us that a couple of
          years ago you spent a summer among
          the primitive San Blas Indians in
          Panama...You wrote a paper on it...

                    STEVE
                 (Surprised)
          Yes, Sir. I did!...I'm flattered
          Dr. Ambrose should remember it.

                    BANKES
          He considered it important enough
          to recommend you as an authority on
          the customs and psychology of the
          tribal Indians - and their language...
          You still remember it?...

                    STEVE
          Yes...Enough to get along...

                    BANKES
          Good.  Come over here...

He walks to the screen around the bed; Camera follows
him; he pushes the screen aside; a figure is lying on
the bed, the head hidden by the doctor, who is bent over
the bed listening to the patient's heart through a
stethoscope; the doctor straightens up - and steps
aside...

Camera zooms in to a C.U. of the man lying on the bed;
it is the Indian we saw hunted and shot in the jungle;
both his shoulders and arms are heavily bandaged; he
looks feverish and delirious...

35.  WIDER ANGLE

The men gather around the bed.

                         BANKES
            How is he, Doctor?

                         DOCTOR
            Barely conscious...I'm afraid he
            won't last long...

                         BANKES
                    (Urgently)
            Mr. Carter.  It is imperative that
            we learn who this man is...where he
            came from!  Can you find out?

      Without a word Steve kneels by the bed; Camera dollies
      in to a CLOSE SHOT:  Steve bends over the Indian.

                         STEVE
                    (Quietly)
            Nueddee...Nueddee...

      There is no response from the Indian

36.   WIDER ANGLE

                         BANKES
            He comes from somewhere in Panama...
            Can you place his tribe?

                         STEVE
            It might be San Blas...I can't be
            sure...

      Gently he touches some markings on the Indians cheeks
      (scars or tatoos.)

                         STEVE
            These markings...I think he is a
            Contoolie...

                         BANKES
            Contoolie?

                         STEVE
            Sort of - witch doctor...

                         BANKES
                 (Looking at Harrison)
            It fits!

                         HARRISON
            Try again...

Steve bends over the Indian.

37. TWO SHOT

                    STEVE
          Nueddee...Nueddee, contoolie!...

Slowly the Indian's eyes turn towards Steve.

38. C.U. BANKES

He is watching tensely.

                    STEVE (O.S.)
          Nueddee...

39. C.U. HARRISON

He, too, is watching; he is puffing away unconsciously
on his pipe...

                    STEVE (O.S.)
          ...Contoolie...Nueddee!...

40. TWO SHOT. STEVE AND INDIAN

                    STEVE
          Nueddee...

Suddenly the Indian's lips begin to move - he is trying
to speak; the sounds come out in faint, sporadic whispers; Steve bends to listen...

41. C.U. BANKES

He bends forward intently...

42. C.U. HARRISON

He is holding his pipe - unnoticed - in front of his
open mouth - he is straining to listen...

43. CLOSE GROUP SHOT

Suddenly the Indian's eyes open wide; he strains to
set up - then he falls back on the bed, exhausted; at
once the doctor begins to examine him; Bankes looks
at him questioningly; the doctor shakes his head; the
men slowly walk away from the bed; only the doctor
remains with the Indian...

44. WIDER ANGLE - DOLLY IN TO GROUP SHOT

                    BANKES
          Did he say anything?  Could you
          make it out?

                    STEVE
                    (Frowning)
          Not very well...He is not a San Blas
          Indian...and yet...he is a Cuna...
          I think he may be from an inland
          tribe...

Bankes turns to Mendez.  In the B.G. the doctor straightens up; he pulls the covers over the face of the Indian -
and places the screen around the bed.

                    BANKES
          How about it?

                    MENDEZ
          It is possible.  The jungle between
          the Canal Zone and Colombia is largely
          unexplored...The Indians are quite
          uncivilized...

                    HARRISON
          Did you understand anything he said?

                    STEVE
          Only two words...One means 'evil'...
          the other means 'thing that flies'...
          maybe bird...'evil bird'...

                    BANKES
                    (Grimly)
          That's it!

                    STEVE
          I don't understand...

Bankes glances at Harrison, who nods imperceptibly.

                    BANKES
          Two days ago this Indian came stumb-
          ling out of the jungle into a small
          Panamanian village...He was more dead
          than alive...The villagers took him
          to an Air Force base in the Zone...
          and he was flown up here at once!

                    STEVE
               But - why??!

Bankes reaches into an open attache case standing on a
chair; he brings out a leather string on which hang
half a dozen small objects; it is the charm necklace
that the Indian wore; Bankes hands it to Steve.

                    BANKES
               Because of - this!

45.  CLOSE TWO SHOT.  BANKES AND STEVE

Steve looks at the necklace in startled astonishment.

                    BANKES
               Your primitive - witch doctor - had
               it around his neck...You see what
               those objects are...

46.  CLOSE SHOT.  NECKLACE IN STEVE'S HANDS

On the leather string are fastened six objects:  A small
radio vacuum tube; a coil; four tooled, small metal
machine parts.

                    STEVE (O.S.)
               A radio vacuum tube!  A coil!...

47.  TWO SHOT - OVERLAPPING

Steve is examining the necklace.

                    STEVE

               ...tooled metal machine parts!

                    BANKES
               Look closer, Mr. Carter!

Steve peers closely at the objects; then he slowly lets
the necklace sink down...

                    STEVE
                    (Frowning)
               The markings...on the tube...they
               look...foreign...
                    (With sudden realization)
               ...Oriental!

He looks with a startled expression at Bankes.

                         BANKES
                       (Seriously)
               Exactly!

There is a knock at the door, Grant opens it...

48.   WIDER ANGLE

      Bankes goes to the door; he confers briefly with one of
      the guards; then he turns to the others.

                         BANKES
                   Frank Duncan of the C.I.A. is wait-
                   ing for us in my office.  We can do
                   nothing further here.  I suggest we
                   leave at once.

                                             DISSOLVE

49.   EXT. NIGHT. L.S.  MAIN ENTRANCE. PENTAGON BUILDING
      (STOCK)

      There is general activity.

50.   INT. NIGHT. COL. BANKES' OFFICE
      CLOSE SHOT.  WALL MAP OF PANAMA

      A hand is pointing to an area in the center of the
      country, half-way between the Canal Zone and the
      Colombian border; a mountain range is indicated on
      the map with the legend:  Maje Mountains...

      Camera dollies out to reveal Steve standing by the map,
      pointing...

      Present in the office are Col. Bankes, Alan Grant, Carlos
      Mendez, Donald Harrison and Frank Duncan; the last is
      a man around fifty years of age; sharp, quick and intelli-
      gent; he is a high official of the C.I.A.; he wears
      civilian clothes.

      Camera dollies out to a MED. SHOT, during:

                         STEVE
                   ...There are several Indian tribes
                   in there - in the jungles of the
                   interior...all of them uncivilized -
                   and pretty savage...The Dariens -
                   the Chocos - the Chucunaques...Like
                   the San Blas they speak a form of
                   Cuna-Cuna - a Chibchan dialect...
                   Somewhere in that area must be the
                   tribe from which the contoolie came...

                              BANKES
               Then that's where the plane crashed!

51.   TWO SHOT.   BANKES AND DUNCAN

                              DUNCAN
               You're quite sure those machine parts came
               from a plane?

                              BANKES
               Positive!  We've had experts examine
               them...Without a doubt they're from a
               recent design aircraft engine - of a
               foreign and unfamiliar make...

52.   WIDER ANGLE

      Duncan walks towards the map and studies it thoughtfully.

                              DUNCAN
               Then - if we are to believe the evidence
               of a necklace worn by this Indian witch
               doctor, an aircraft from a foreign -
               possibly hostile country penetrated our
               radar warning screen...and crashed in the
               jungle!...

                              HARRISON
                              (To Bankes)
               Yes, Sir...There is a chain of radar
               stations - in operation twenty-four
               hours a day - It is an impenetrable
               system...

                              HARRISON
                              (Pointedly)
               Supposedly impenetrable!...Has there
               been any recent unexplained radar
               sightings?  U.F.O.'s?...

                              BANKES
               None!

      Duncan turns to Steve; he looks grave.

53.   TWO SHOT.   DUNCAN AND STEVE

                              DUNCAN
               Mr. Carter...I'm sure you realize
               the gravity of this situation...

                              STEVE
                              (soberly)
               I do...

                    DUNCAN
          If our Radar Warning System has been
          penetrated, we must know how - by
          whom!  It could conceivably be done
          again!

                    STEVE
          I see...

                    DUNCAN
          It will be the mission of the C.I.A.
          to find these answers...We're sending an
          Investigation Team to Panama - headed
          by Agent Grant...We want you to go along!

                    STEVE
          Me!

                    DUNCAN
          We know your training and field work
          make you very well qualified...

                    STEVE
          Qualified - for what?...

                    DUNCAN
          Grant will have to infiltrate deep
          into the jungle...deal with the
          primitive Indians...He'll need
          someone along who knows them - an
          interpreter and someone who can
          take care of himself - when the
          goings rough...You're it, Mr. Carter!

                    STEVE
                    (Troubled)
          I want to help, of course...But - it
          would be a rather bad time for me to
          have to leave just now...There are a
          couple of personal matters I must
          straighten out...I'll need a little
          time...

                    DUNCAN
          There is no time!  If you agree to
          go with Grant - you'll be on a plane
          for the Canal Zone in less than two
          hours!

Steve looks startled; he is thinking hard.

                    DUNCAN
          The choice is yours, Mr. Carter...
          We are not forcing you...And one
          thing more...

                         STEVE
          Yes?...

                         DUNCAN
          There may be danger...and no glory!
          ...But you have a chance to render
          your country a great service!

Steve stands silent; he frowns in worried concentration.

54.   WIDER ANGLE

Harrison goes up to Steve.

                         HARRISON
          I wonder if you realize how vital
          the Panama Canal is to our country's
          defense...Especially in the event
          of armed conflict...?

                         STEVE
          Of course I do...

55.   TWO SHOT.  HARRISON AND STEVE

Harrison turns to the wall map; he points.

                         HARRISON
             There is the Gatun Dam and Locks...

Camera dollies in across the men to a CLOSE SHOT of the
Canal Zone Map; Harrison's hand points to the Gatun Locks
and Dam...

                         HARRISON
          ...A successful attack here...One
          well-placed bomb...

56.   CLOSE SHOT.  HARRISON - OVERLAPPING

He turns to face Steve.

                         HARRISON
          ...and the entire Gatun Lake would
          drain dry - making the Canal com-
          pletely useless - for at least two
          years!

57.   TWO SHOT.  HARRISON AND STEVE.  OVERLAPPING

                         HARRISON
          Do you have any idea of the military
          implications of that?

Steve stands silent and serious for a moment; then he
looks up.

> STEVE
> (Resolutely)
> Is there a phone I can use?

58.   INT. NIGHT. JANET'S ROOM.   CLOSE SHOT.   PHONE

It rings; Janet's hand comes into the picture and picks
up the phone: Camera widens and follows to a C.U.   JANET.

> JANET
> (On phone)
> Hello?...Steve!...
> (She brightens)
> You've thought it over!  You...

She stops suddenly - interrupted...

Camera slowly pulls out to a M.C.U. of Janet; she is
sitting in her bed; she is clad in a lacy nightgown;
she has been reading; she listens - and a small frown
begins to cloud her lovely face.

> JANET
> (On phone)
> ...Wait a minute, Steve!  What's this
> all about?  How long will you be gone?...
> Why all the mystery?

59.   INT. C.U.   STEVE

He is talking on the phone.

> STEVE
> (On phone)
> I'm sorry I can't tell you more about
> it, Jan...But it's a confidential
> matter...vital to our government...

60.   C.U. JANET

> JANET
> (On phone)
> Alright, Steve...Just tell me one
> thing:  Has that - trip of yours -
> anything to do with anthropology?
> (She listens; she looks
> displeased; grimly)
> Well - it looks like you've made
> your final decision, then, doesn't
> it?!...

61.  C.U. STEVE

                    STEVE
                  (On phone)
           No...Look, Jan...we still have a
           lot to talk over...

62.  C.U. JANET

                    JANET
                  (On phone)
           We'll talk it over, then - tomorrow
           - or not at all!  Goodbye, Steve...

63.  C.U. STEVE

                    STEVE
                  (On phone)
           Jan!  Listen to me, Jan...Jan..!

64.  CLOSE SHOT. JANET

     She is sitting in bed looking at the receiver in her hand;
     then she hangs up; she picks up her book thoughtfully -
     then she makes a small, impatient gesture of annoyance...

65.  INT. NIGHT. DUNCAN'S OFFICE.  MED. SHOT

     Duncan, Harrison, Bankes, Grant and Mendez talking
     quietly among themselves are waiting for Steve's re-
     turn.  The door opens and Steve enters; he stops just
     inside the door; the men all turn towards him expect-
     antly.

66.  C.U.  DUNCAN

     He looks with grave expectance at Steve.

67.  C.U. HARRISON

     He puffs on his pipe.

68.  C.U. BANKES

     He looks impatient.

69.  C.U. GRANT

     He watches Steve with curious appraisal.

70.  CLOSE SHOT.  STEVE

     He looks from one man to another.  Then...

STEVE

I'm ready!!

DISSOLVE

71. L.S. SUNRISE SHOT. U.S. AIR FORCE PLANE (B-52) SHOT FROM FOLLOW PLANE. (STOCK)

The big jet plane is flying above the clouds, R to L; the sun is rising, turning the white, convoluted cloud blanket into a wooly quilt of red, pink and gold...

72. M.L.S. DAY. THE PLANE. SHOT FROM FOLLOW PLANE (STOCK)

The plane (B-52) is flying R to L over the Panama Canal Zone; it banks to prepare for a landing.

73. AERIAL SHOT. DAY. (STOCK)

Viewed from the plane flying R to L we see the Gatun Lake, the Dam and Locks.

74 to 80. AERIAL SHOTS. DAY (STOCK)

Various shots of interesting activities around the Gatun Locks...A large ship is passing through one of the lock chambers; six "electric mules" - towing locomotives running on cog tracks on the lock walls on both sides of the chamber - can be seen slowly moving the vessel through...In another chamber the huge lock gates are closing - and the water starts to rush into the chamber, filling it...

81. EXT. DAY. ALBROOK FIELD, A.F.B., PANAMA CANAL ZONE, HQ CARIBBEAN COMMAND
L.S. LANDING FIELD. (STOCK)

A plane (B-52) is landing on the runway.

82. EXT. DAY. ALBROOK FIELD RUNWAY. L.S. (STOCK)

A plane (B-52) is taxiing towards camera.

83. EXT. DAY. SIGN. CLOSE SHOT. (STOCK)

The sign is over a hangar, gate or administration building; it identifies the location as:

ALBROOK FIELD AIR FORCE BASE
PANAMA CANAL ZONE
H.Q. CARIBBEAN COMMAND

84. EXT. DAY. SHOTS. (STOCK)

Various interesting and colorful scenes typical of the different activities on the base.

85. EXT. DAY. M.L.S. ALBROOK FIELD ADMINISTRATION BUILDING.

Two Air Force jeeps drive up before the main entrance;
three men get out; they are Steve, Grant, and C.I.A.
Agent, Tom Warnecke, a young man in his late twenties.
The men enter the building as the drivers take off
in the jeeps.

                                    DISSOLVE

86. INT. DAY.  CLOSE SHOT. DOOR

On it is the legend:

                    A-2
              ROBERT S. WARD
              Maj. U.S.A.F.

87. INT. DAY. WARD'S OFFICE. CLOSE SHOT, WARD

The office of the Air Intelligence Officer, Major
Robert S. Ward - a man in his late thirties, quick,
matter-of-fact, without humor - is functionally
furnished; maps and pictures identify it with the
Panama Canal Zone.  Ward is standing behind his desk;
Camera pulls back to a MED. SHOT including Steve,
Grant, and Warnecke sitting in front of the desk,
during:

                    WARD
              ....Washington has already briefed
              me on the importance of your mission,
              Mr. Grant...Any assistance Air
              Intelligence can give you - just say
              the word...

                    GRANT
              What about radio communication?  Tom
              Warnecke here...
                   (He indicates Warnecke
                   with a nod)
              ...is our radio-man.

                    WARD
              A twenty-four-hour contact station
              will be set up for you...

                    WARNECKE
              Good...

Ward picks up a sheet of paper from his desk and hands
it to Warnecke, during:

                    WARD
          You will use code - no voice
          transmission...Messages will be
          sent in cipher...double transpo-
          sition...Here are the key words...
          easy to remember...

Warnecke reads the words written on the paper Ward
handed him.

                    WARNECKE
          'Sarcophagus' - 'Formaldehyde'....
                    (He grins)
          Who's my contact?  The local
          undertaker?!

Steve grins; Ward reaches for the paper; he takes it.

                    WARD
                    (He is not amused)
          The words were selected for their
          letter combinations...

                    WARNECKE
          Of course...

He winks at Steve, who grins back; a buzzer on Ward's
desk sounds; Ward picks up the phone.

                    WARD
                    (On phone)
          Yes?...Send him in.

He hangs up.

                    WARD
           C.I.A. requested that Panama be
          represented on your Investigation
          Team...Since Panama has no army,
          navy or  air force, the Government
          has chosen an officer of the National
          Police Force to accompany you...

                    GRANT
          Fine...

                    WARD
          Lt. Juan Herrara...I know Herrara
          personally...He is a good officer...
          He is already attending to your
          supplies and cargadores...

The door opens and a young Panamanian in the uniform
of a Lieutenant in the National Police Force enters;
it is Lt. Juan Herrara; the men all turn towards him.

88.  MED. SHOT. HERRARA

> HERRARA
> All is ready, Major Ward...We can
> leave for the jungle within the
> hour...

DISSOLVE

89.  AERIAL SHOT. DAY. JUNGLE (STOCK)

Below stretches a sea of green as far as the eye can
see; a narrow river winds its way through the wild
tropical jungle;

90.  EXT. DAY. L.S.  JUNGLE RIVER

Two small boats or canoes are making their way up-
stream; in #1 boat are Steve, Grant and two native
cargadores; in #2 boat, following #1, are Herrara,
Warnecke and another native cargador; the men are all
clad in civilian, tropical khaki clothing; the cargadores wear colorful native dress; in both of the boats
several amall cases and packs of supplies can be seen.

91.  MED. SHOT FROM LEAD CAMERA BOAT TO TWO SMALL BOATS

They are paddling up the river stream

92.  CLOSE TWO SHOT.  STEVE AND GRANT

They are paddling rythmically.

93.  CLOSE SHOT. CANOE BOW.

It is slicing through the water against the current;
the water swirls and foams around the bow - rushing
L. to R.

MATCH

94.  CLOSE SHOT.  SHARP ROCK IN WATER

The water swirls and foams around the rock - rushing
L. to R.

95.  EXT. DAY. L.S.  RIVER RAPIDS.

The river has narrowed down considerably; it comes
rushing down the rocky rapids; it is no longer navi-
gable; the two boats are being beached nearby; the

95. CONTINUED                                          26.

supplies are being unloaded...

96.  CLOSER ANGLE

The men are pulling the canoes up on the muddy river
bank; they are carrying the supply cases and packs
from the little boats; Steve takes a heavy case and
starts towards the bank...

97.  CLOSE SHOT. STEVE'S FEET.

Steve is walking heavily through the soft, wet mud
and sand; his booted feet make wet footprints in the
mud - going L. to R...

MATCH

98.  CLOSE SHOT. STEVE'S FEET.

They are making wet footprints in the mud of a small
jungle swamp - going L to R...

99.  EXT. DAY. JUNGLE SWAMP.  WIDER ANGLE

The little expedition is making its way through the
jungle; they are just leaving a swampy area; they walk
in single file l to R;  Grant is in the lead, followed
by Steve, Herrara and the Three cargadores; Warnecke
brings up the rear.  The cargadores carry the supply
cases; the others carry packs on their backs and are
armed with rifles...

100.  MED. SHOT

The men file past the camera in M.C.U's L to R; first
Grant, then Steve and Herrara, then the cargadores;
as the cargadores walk past, camera pans down a little
to feature the colorful designs on the men's native
shirt/blouses; the last cargador walks very close to
camera presenting in a CLOSE SHOT a picture of blazing
color and design:  The bright red of Panama's hibiscus
flower; the yellow of the trumpet-vine blooms; the blue
of the tropical seas; the green of hills and trees;
the orange and brown of nuts and fruits; the gold of
the sun...a riot of design and color...

MATCH

101.  CLOSE SHOT. MACAW.

The big bird is a riot of design and color; it is
perched on a branch looking directly into camera; it
bristles its red, blue, yellow and green feathers and
screeches raucously...

102. WIDER ANGLE.

The Macaw (and possibly other birds) take off...

103. SHOT. TOUCAN.

The brilliantly colored bird flaps away among the trees...

104. SHOT. IGUANA.

The huge, nearly six-foot-long land lizard sprints away stiff-legged through the jungle underbrush...

105. SHOT. FAMILY OF WILD BOARS.

They are running away - tails in the air...

106. EXT. DAY. JUNGLE. MED. WIDE SHOT.

The men are making their way through the jungle growth; from their appearance they have obviously been on the go for some time now, and the going is rough. Steve is in the lead; he is using a machete - hacking away at a thick stand of bamboo.

107. CLOSE SHOT. STEVE.

His machete is cutting into the bamboo.

108. CLOSE SHOT. MACHETE. CUTTING BAMBOO.

The sharp machete hacks into a couple of thick bamboo stalks - once, twice, and it cuts through; the bamboo crashes down...

MATCH

109. CLOSE SHOT. MACHETE. CUTTING LIANES.

The machete hacks into a knot of hanging lianes - once, twice, and it cuts through; the lianes crash down...

110. EXT. DAY. JUNGLE ANIMAL TRAIL. WIDER ANGLE

The trail is overgrown with heavy lianes; the men are hacking their way through; Herrara is in the lead using the machete.

111. MED. CLOSE SHOT. HERRARA

He is hacking away at the lianes.

112.   SHOT. JAGUAR.

The animal is standing on a tree limb; in the distance
can be heard the sounds of the expedition cutting
through the lianes...Suddenly the jaguar takes off...

113.   SHOT.  MULE DEER

It is standing, alertly listening; the sounds of the men
approaching can be heard; suddenly the deer takes off...

114.   SHOT.  GROUP OF PECCARIES.

They trot away through the jungle, as the sounds of the
men intrude upon their browsing...

DISSOLVE

(NOTE:  The preceeding brief se uence is flexible and
should be designed in the field to take best advantage
of location and available shot interest; more jungle
scenes and wild animal shots may be added.  The
sequence is included in this form here to show how
the passing of time and distance should be conveyed
by match cuts in the film.)

115.   EXT. DAY.  JUNGLE TRAIL.  MED. WIDE SHOT

The men are walking along the animal trail; Grant and
Steve in the lead, followed by Herrara and the others.
Suddenly Herrara points off...

HERRARA
Grant!...Over there!...

The men stop; they all look in the direction Herrara
is pointing.

116.   L.S.  JUNGLE TRAIL  HERRARA'S P.O.V.

At the edge of the trail a little ahead is a large,
brown mound; a heap of white bones lies next to it;
the rib cage can be made out clearly.

117.   MED. SHOT.  THE TRAIL

The men are looking towards the skeleton; Warnecke
joins Grant, Steve and Herrara.

GRANT
Let's have a look...

They start towards the skeleton.

118.   THE JUNGLE.  HEAD-ON SHOT.  THE FOUR MEN.

They are walking directly at Camera to a MED. FOUR SHOT:
they stop and look down...Camera sinks down to show
the mound of an ant hill in the F.G.; next to the ant
hill lies the stripped skeleton of a wild boar with
ants still swarming all over it.  Camera holds on a
shot across the clean-picked boar skeleton in F.G.
to the four men in the B.G.

                    GRANT
          Wild boar...Those ants sure picked
          it clean...

                    WARNECKE
          What's that?...

He bends down and pries loose a small object imbedded
in the hip bone of the boar; he straightens up and shows
it to the others.

119.   CLOSE FOUR SHOT.

Warnecke is holding up the little object for all to see.

                    STEVE
               It's an arrowhead...

120.   C.U. ARROWHEAD IN WARNECKE'S HAND.

It is slender, pointed and about three inches long,
and has several sharp hooks along one side.

121.   FOUR SHOT

                    WARNECKE
          Cuna?...

                    STEVE
          Yes...

                    GRANT
          We're on the right track...That
          boar couldn't have run too far with
          a thing like that sticking in it...

Warnecke has been examining the arrowhead curiously.

                    WARNECKE
          What's it made of?  It isn't metal -
          but it's mighty heavy...

                    STEVE
          The Indians in here don't use metal
          in their weapons...That's wood...
          from the Guaiacum Tree...one of the
          hardest woods in the world...won't
          split...

                    WARNECKE
          I think I'll take it back to Duncan...
          make a nice toothpick!...

                    STEVE
                 (Casually)
          I guess it isn't poisoned...

Warnecke looks up with a start.

                    WARNECKE
          Poisoned!?

He holds the arrowhead out from him - gingerly - with
two fingers.

                    STEVE
          Sure!  Most of the Indian arrows and
          blowgun darts are dipped in poison.

                    WARNECKE
          Yeah?

                    STEVE
                 (Enjoying himself)
          They've even got a very special kind...
          they let a pitful of poisonous snakes
          sink their fangs in a pig's liver until
          it's saturated with venom...Then, when
          the liver has rotted into a putrid,
          poisoned mess - they dip their arrows
          in it!

122.  CLOSE SHOT.  WARNECKE

He is looking at the arrowhead in his fingers with a
comical look of horrified disgust; he opens his fingers
and lets the arrowhead fall to the ground.

                    WARNECKE
          Not very civilized, are they?!

123.  GROUP SHOT.

                    HERRARA
                 (With a grin)
          We say in Panama...If you go 50 miles
          into the jungle, you go 500 years back
          in time!

                        WARNECKE
                50 miles, eh?  And we've come over
                70 by now...Where does that leave
                us?...

Steve picks up the arrowhead; he tosses it to Warnecke.

                        STEVE
                Here...Take it...That one isn't poisoned...
                or the boar couldn't have run off...

Grant has been looking ahead.

                        GRANT
                There's a small clearing up ahead...
                We'll make camp there for the night...
                        (To Herrara)
                Juan...Tell the boys...

Herrara goes off towards the cargadores; Grant looks
speculatively down at the boar remains...

Camera pans down to a CLOSE SHOT of the clean-picked,
ant ridden boar rack.

124.    EXT. DAY. AFTERNOON.  L.S.  JUNGLE CLEARING.

At one end of the little clearing the three cargadores
are putting down their burdens, supervised by Herrara;
a little distance away Grant, Steve, and Warnecke
stand talking; they have put down their packs and
leaned their rifles against them; they are consulting
a map held by Grant.

125.    MED. THREE SHOT.  GRANT STEVE, AND WARNECKE.

                        GRANT
                We've made pretty good time...nine
                days out - and we're right about -
                here...

                        WARNECKE
                We're making time, alright...But
                we haven't found a thing yet...
                        (He holds up his arrowhead)
                except this...

Suddenly - without warning - a long, slender spear
comes hurtling through the air, burying itself in
the ground mere inches in front of the three men to
stand there - quivering ominously...

The startled men react - they look up...

126. WIDER ANGLE.  THE CLEARING

The members of the little expedition are looking up in
startled fear; and all around them - from the dense
jungle - step a horde of savage looking Indians to
form a ring around them; in their hands they hold bows,
their strings taut upon cruelly pointed and barbed
arrows, spears and blowguns at the ready; silent and
menacing they surround the party...

127. MED. THREE SHOT.  GRANT, STEVE AND WARNECKE.

Warnecke makes a move to grab his gun, but Steve  stops
him imperatively.

                          STEVE
                    Don't move!

128. ANOTHER ANGLE FEATURING HERRARA AND THE CARGADORES.
     GRANT, STEVE AND WARNECKE ARE IN B.G.

With a short cry Herrara draws his gun from his belt...
But before he can even raise it, there is a series of
soft thuds - as several long, needle sharp darts shoot
into his neck...With a hideous shriek Herrara grabs
at the wounds - and falls to the ground - dead!

The three cargadores stare at him for a split second
in stunned horror; then - as one man - they turn and
bolt into the jungle.

129. ANOTHER ANGLE FEATURING GRANT, STEVE AND WARNECKE.

In the B.G. the cargadores are fleeing - disappearing
into the jungle; the three men make a move towards
the fallen Herrara - the the menacing, silent Indians
close in around them.

130. CLOSE PAN SHOT.  INDIANS.

Ominously scowling they stand immobile, silent, coldly
staring at the three white men.

131. CLOSE THREE SHOT.  GRANT, STEVE AND WARNECKE.

Grimly they stand stock still.

132. ANOTHER CLOSE SHOT.  INDIANS

Their faces look fierce and ruthless; they seem to be
waiting...Suddenly - from the jungle - echoes a
hideous screem...

33.

133. CLOSE THREE SHOT.  GRANT, STEVE AND WARNECKE

They react in shock; another scream rings out - and
another...The three men get a hard glint in their
eyes as they realize the fate of their three cargadores.

134. WIDER ANGLE.

The three men stand stock still ringed by the motionless
Indians; suddenly the ring opens up - and a man steps
through.  He wears a huge headdress, dripping with
gaudily colored feathers; around his neck hangs a
necklace of bones; he carries a weirdly shaped calabash
in his hand; it is Terui, a contoolie...

135. CLOSER SHOT ACROSS GRANT, STEVE AND WARNECKE TO TERUI.

For a suspenseful moment Terui stands glaring at the
three white men; then he suddenly barks:

                    TERUI
          Setagi!...Setagi!...

He turns on his heel and starts to walk away.  Steve
turns to his companions.

                    STEVE
          He wants us to go with him...

                    GRANT
          We have no choice...

136. WIDER ANGLE.

Grant, Steve and Warnecke start to follow Terui, while
the menacing warriors stonily watch them - and then
fall in close behind as they enter the jungle.

                              DISSOLVE

137. EXT. DAY. L.S.  LARGE JUNGLE CLEARING.

The clearing shows signs of inhabitation; from the
jungle Terui, Grant, Steve and Warnecke emerge into
the clearing, followed by the Indians.  They stop...

138. CLOSE ANGLE - FOUR SHOT

Terui points ahead with his calabash.

                    TERUI
                  (In Cuna)
          Go!...

The men look off, where he points; they react.

> GRANT
> Looks like we've arrived...

> WARNECKE
> Yeah! But - where?...

139. L.S. P.O.V. THREE MEN

At the other end of the clearing stands a fairly large
hut; its walls are made of bamboo poles set close together and laced with lianes or vine ropes; the roof
is thickly thatched with dried palm leaves; in front
of it an overhang forms a sort of patio. Nobody is
in sight.

140. FOUR SHOT

Again Terui points at the hut.

> TERUI
> (In Cuna)
> Go...Go!...

> STEVE
> He's telling us to go to the
> hut.

> GRANT
> Come on...

The three men start off.

141. WIDER ANGLE

Grant, Steve and Warnecke are walking towards the hut;
behind them Terui and all the Indians - strung out in
a line - remain standing in utter silence and immo-
bility.

142. THREE SHOT

The three men are walking towards the hut; they are
almost there; suddenly they stop...

143. MED. SHOT. THE HUT.

The door opens; out steps a girl! She sees the three
men - and stops dead in surprise; she is about twenty-
two years of age; a lovely latin beauty with dark,
expressive eyes; it is Nenita Arias (Nita). She is
clad in a simple shirt or blouse and tropical slacks.

144. CLOSE THREE SHOT.   GRANT, STEVE AND WARNECKE.

The men react in astonishment.

145. REVERSE ANGLE.   ACROSS THREE MEN TO NITA

The girl is standing just outside the door; before
either she or the men can recover from their mutual
astonishment at seeing each other, a man steps from
the hut; he is tall, muscular and erect, around forty,
with close-cropped blond hair; he is dressed in gray
tropicals and carries two guns strapped to his belt.
It is Gregor Stepan - he is startled at the sight
of Grant, Steve and Warnecke; he looks grimly danger-
our - like a cornered puma...

Nita is just about to say something, but Stepan takes
her arm.

                    STEPAN
                (Quickly; firmly)
          Cuidadoso!

He nods towards the door; without a word the girl goes
inside; Stepan turns his attention on the three men
standing before him; he has regained his composure.

146. MED. SHOT

                    STEPAN
                (Pleasantly)
          Bievnenida, senores...Me llamo
          Gregor Stepan...

                    GRANT
                (Stepping forward)
          I am Alan Grant...This is Steven
          Carter...Tom Warnecke...

                    STEPAN
            (With sudden added interest)
            (He speaks with an unidenti-
                fiable accent)
          Americans!...What brings you here?

                    STEVE
          We were attacked by the Indians...
          They killed one of our companions...
          our cargadores...and took us here...

                    STEPAN
                (Grimly)
          They tolerate no strangers...They
          are a warlike tribe...You are lucky
          they did not kill you all!...

He looks towards the Indians standing silently at the other end of the clearing; he raises his voice.

                    STEPAN
                  (Sharply)
          Terui!

147.  WIDER ANGLE.  INCLUDING THE INDIANS.  OVERLAPPING

                    STEPAN
                  (In Cuna)
              Leave us!

Immediately the Indians and Terui turn and disappear into the jungle.

148.  FOUR SHOT

The three men look after the Indians with a mixture of relief and amazement; Steve turns to Stepan.

                    STEVE
              (With puzzled interest)
          You seem to have quite a way with
          them...

                    STEPAN
              (He smiles mirthlessly)
          We have - an understanding...

                    GRANT
          Perhaps you could help us get our
          weapons back - our supplies...We had
          to leave everything...

                    STEVE
          ...And take care of Juan...the man
          they killed...

                    STEPAN
          Perhaps...
              (He turns to the hut)
          Come in...We will talk...

They start for the hut.

149.  INT. HUT. MED. SHOT - DOOR.

The hut is quite spacious; it is crudely but adequately furnished; another door leads to a back room; there is a large table, several chairs, and in one corner stands a bamboo gun rack with several rifles, some of them with telescopic sight; two hammocks are hanging from the wall on one side.  The door opens and Stepan enters, followed by Grant, Steve and Warnecke; Camera widens

                                            (CONT.)

and follows to see a man sitting at the table facing
the door; he is in his fifties, but appears to be older;
he is greying and tired looking; he wears khaki tropicals and is unarmed; it is Emilio Manuel Arias; behind
him stands Nita.

> STEPAN
> May I present my partner, Emilio
> Manuel Arias...and his daughter,
> Nenita...

Grant, Steve and Warnecke acknowledge the introduction;
Arias bows his head in greeting.

> STEPAN
> (To Arias)
> These gentlemen are - Americans...
> (Arias reacts sharply; Stepan
> turns to the three men)
> Please make yourselves comfortable...

They do.

150.   TWO SHOT.   GRANT AND STEPAN

They are watching each other closely; it is like a
cautious, verbal fencing match:  Question thrust -
answer parry...thrust - parry...In the distance the
sounds of native drums and chanting begins.

> GRANT
> You have been in the jungle long?

> STEPAN
> Many months...

> GRANT
> We didn't expect to find any white
> men this deep in the interior...

> STEPAN
> My partner is a geologist...I am
> a mining engineer...

> GRANT
> Mining?

> STEPAN
> It has long been known there is
> gold and silver in these mountain...
> and you...?

151.   MED. SHOT - OVERLAPPING

Stepan looks around at the men.

                         STEPAN
              You too are prospecting?

                          STEVE
              No - as a matter of fact...

Grant quickly interrupts.

                          GRANT
              ...As a matter of fact - we are
              scientists - anthropologists...
              We had hoped to establish contact
              with the primitive Indians of the
              mountains...

                         WARNECKE
              But not quite the way it happened...
              I suppose we owe our lives to your
              presence here...

                         STEPAN
              These Indians have had virtually
              no contact with white men - perhaps
              since the Spanish conquistadores...

                          GRANT
                     (Regarding Stepan)
              You are - Russian?...

                         STEPAN
                     (With a thin smile)
              You are observing.  I am Czeck...
              I left my country many years ago...

152.    ANOTHER ANGLE - FEATURING DOOR

        Suddenly the door bursts open- and a weird apparition
        of a figure leaps into the hut - rattling a calabash
        furiously; his face is painted and he is decked out
        it gaudy feathers and cloth; it is Terui...

153.    TWO SHOT.  GRANT AND WARNECKE

        The react.

154.    C.U.  STEVE

        He reacts.

155.    MED. SHOT

        Terui suddenly stops his rattling - and points drama-
        tically at Nita; without a word the girl gets up;

155.   CONTINUED

she takes a colorful shawl from a hook on the wall;
drapes it over her head and shoulders - and follows
Terui from the hut; the three Americans look after
them; then Grant turns to Stepan; Stepan smiles.

                    STEPAN
          It is the night for the Ceremony
          of the Haircutting...

                    WARNECKE
             (He nods after the depart-
               ing Terui)
          Some barber!...

                    STEPAN
          Terui is the Contoolie - the
          native witch doctor...He presides
          at the ceremony...

                    WARNECKE
          Cutting hair?...

                    STEPAN
          It's the celebration of the
          Transition of a native girl - from
          girlhood to womanhood...The Indians
          admire Nita's hair...They always
          ask her to participate...As a good
          omen...

                    WARNECKE
          What do you know...

                    STEPAN
             (With studied unconcern)
          I should have thought - by your
          profession - that you'd know a
          little about such customs...

                    WARNECKE
             (Thinking fast)
          Me?...I'm no scientist!  I'm just -
          a technician...

Stepan looks at Warnecke speculatively.

                    STEPAN
             (Shrewdly)
          It is a very interesting ceremony...
          as "anthropologists" I'm sure you would
          like to watch it?...

STEVE
(Enthusiastically)
Yes...We would...

Stepan looks at Steve quickly; his eyes narrow almost
imperceptibly.

STEPAN
Good.  There are a few hours of
preparations first...Then I'll take
you there myself...

CUT TO.

156.  EXT. NIGHT.  NATIVE VILLAGE JUNGLE CLEARNING. L.S.
      THROUGH THE FLAMES OF A HUGE FIRE TO INDIANS DANCING.

157.  THE CEREMONY OF HAIR CUTTING

The ceremony will be staged on location.  It is the
celebration of the transition of a native girl from
girlhood into womanhood.

The ceremony is presided over by Terui, the contoolie,
a young Indian girl is stripped of most of her clothes,
and placed in a large hole previously dug in a corner
of the ceremonial place; a stockade of palm and banana
leaves is backing it; the hole is filled with earth
and sand, until the girl is utterly covered to the
shoulders...

Accompanied by chanting, dancing and the music of
drums, rattles and reed pipes - by the light of the
huge fire the ceremony proceeds...The girl is sprink-
led with water; then, placing a half of a calabash
over her head, a small piece of her long hair is
burned off with a red hot ember from the fire, and
ceremoniously buried in the sand - until the girl's
head is covered only by short tufts of hair...The
first tuft is being singed off by Nita, who then
joins the others watching the ceremony...

At the end of the rites the girl is released - a woman!

INTERCUT.  GROUP SHOT - SPECTATORS

Stepan, Nita, Grant and Steve, with Warnecke and Arias
are watching the ceremony; Stepan looks speculatively
at Grant.

STEPAN
(Thoughtfully)
Being an anthropologist, Mr. Grant...
I'm sure you know the symbolism of
this ceremony...?

                    GRANT
                   (Uneasy)
            Yes...Of course...

                    STEPAN
            (With studied unimportance)
         Terui wasn't too clear, when he
         tried to explain it to me...

He looks intently expectant at Grant and Steve; Grant
looks uncomfortable - Steve grins...

                    STEVE
         It's quite easy to understand, really...
         The burning and burying symbolize all the
         trials and troubles the girl will have
         to meet as an adult...The singing and
         dancing represent the pleasures that
         await her!...Quite simple...

                    STEPAN
                 (Thoughtfully)
         Yes...Quite simple...

Steve turns to look at Stepan.

                    STEVE
         When this is over I suppose they
         have their chicha party?

Stepan looks disappointed; Grant relieved.

                    STEPAN
         They do...

                    WARNECKE
         Chicha!?

                    STEVE
         It's a concoction of fermented
         juices - packs quite a wallop!...

158.   THE CEREMONY.

The ceremony is nearing its end.

159.   ANOTHER ANGLE. L.S.

Terui is helping the girl up - when suddenly a small,
dark figure  bursts from the jungle, races into the
clearing, and leaps over the dying fire!...  As he
runs past Terui, the contoolie suddenly reaches out
and grabs him...Instantly the noise of the celebration
stops; there is a deadly silence...But it is harshly

broken by the sounds of many men crashing through the
jungle - and all at once into the clearing storms a
dozen men carrying rifles in their hands!  They are
all white men; all are clad in like grey uniforms -
and on their feet are big, heavy, black boots!

160.  CLOSE SHOT.  FEATURING STEPAN, GRANT AND STEVE

Grant and Steve look startled; Stepan glares furiously
at the sinister tableau!

161.  L.S.

For a brief moment the frightened natives stand looking
at the grim, menacing men; then - as one - they flee
into the jungle...Everyone except the young boy, who
came from the thicket, and who is held back by Terui.

162.  TWO SHOT.  TERUI AND BOY

The Indian boy is about 16 years of age; it is Eneepe;
he is struggling in Terui's grip; his eyes spark with
defiance and hate.

163.  MED. L.S.

A man detaches himself from the line of menacing soldiers
and walks towards Stepan; he is a brutish, cruel looking fellow about 35 years of age; it is Varnoff.  Stepan
steps forward to meet him; Arias and Nita stand with
each other; Grant, Steve and Warnecke instinctively
draw together, watching the quick developments with
incredulous shock...

                    STEPAN
         Varnoff!  What is this!?  Explain!...

                    VARNOFF
         The boy, Colonel...He got out...

164.  THREE SHOT.  GRANT, STEVE AND WARNECKE

Steve and Warnecke both look at Grant, stunned...Grant
frowns in concentration.

                    STEPAN (O S.)
         Idiot!  Take him back!  Tie
         him up!

Steve, Grant and Warnecke turn again towards Stepan,
they react...

43.

165.  MED. SHOT

Stepan is facing the three men; he has drawn one of
his guns; he is aiming it at the men almost casually.
In the B.G. two of the soldiers take Eneepe from
Terui and march him off...

                    STEPAN
               (With icy pleasantry)
          I think I must have a little talk
          with our guests, now...
                    (Brusquely)
          Varnoff!  Take your men...Get Mr.
          Grant's weapon and supplies...Terui
          will show you where they are...We
          will be at the hut...
                    (He turns to Arias)
          Emilio - lead the way!

They start off.

                                   DISSOLVE

166.  INT. NIGHT.  ST PAN'S HUT.  MED. SHOT

Grant, Steve and Warnecke are standing against one
wall; Stepan, gun in hand, is facing them at a little
distance, sitting nonchalantly at the edge of the
table.  Off to his side stand Arias, also with a gun,
and beside him is Nita.

                    STEPAN
          ...You're quite right, Mr. Grant...
          We are not prospectors!...But them,
          neither do I believe that you are
          anthropologists!...

                    GRANT
          You have troops here - supplies...
          Why?...Who are you?!

Stepan grins unpleasantly.

                    STEPAN
          Let us just say that I am - a
          salesman!

The three men react.

                    STEVE
          Your man called you - Colonel...

                         STEPAN
             Col. Gregor Stepan - retired.

                         GRANT
             What are you selling, Colonel?

                         STEPAN
             I ask the questions, Mr. Grant!

167.   ANOTHER ANGLE

       Suddenly the door opens and Varnoff enters; he is
       carrying Warnecke's radio; he places it on the table
       next to Stepan.

                         VARNOFF
             Here...Look at this...

       Stepan nods for Varnoff to cover the prisoners; Varnoff
       takes out his gun, he smirks lecherously at Nita; the
       girl looks away in angry disgust (plant for later seq.);
       Stepan looks the radio over; he gets a grim, ugly
       expression on his face...

                         STEPAN
                   (He reads on the radio)
             U.S. ARMY!

       He turns to the three men.

                         STEPAN
                   (Ominously)
             Why do you carry U.S. Army equip-
             ment?

                         WARNECKE
             Surpluss material...the best
             available...Real bargains...

       Stepan looks threatening.

                         STEPAN
             I think maybe now I ask some
             questions!...
                   (He barks)
             Who sent you here?

                         GRANT
             We told you...We are...

                         STEPAN
                   (Interrupting)
             I do not believe you!...With whom
             are you in radio contact?

                         GRANT
              The Museum Authorities...In
              Panama City...

                         STEPAN
              We'll see...

He pushes the radio on the table towards the three men.

                         STEPAN
              Who of you is the regular radio
              operator?...

Involuntarily Warnecke reacts; Stepan notices with
satinfaction...

                         STEPAN
              Ah, yes...The "technician"...You
              will send a message...

                         WARNECKE
              I have no intentions of sending
              anything...

                         STEPAN
              You will send a message saying
              you are all well...and - and that
              you are headed for the coast...

He gets up; he walks closer to Warnecke; Camera dollies
in to a CLOSER SHOT.

                         STEPAN
              And don't try to be clever...I
              know morse code myself!

                         WARNECKE
              Then send it yourself!

                         STEPAN
              No.  Not yet!  You!  Your friends in
              Panama are used to your fist!  Send
              the message...

Warnecke looks at him defiantly.

                         STEPAN
              You will also tell them that you
              have been bitten on your right hand
              by an insect...Your hand is swelling!
              ...They won't expect to recognize your
              touch in subsequent transmissions!...
              Go ahead!

                        WARNECKE
            And set it up so you can send any
            message you like about us yourself
            later on!  Not me!

                        STEPAN
                  Send it!

Warnecke doesn't move; Stepan raises his gun; still
Warnecke doesn't move...

                        STEPAN
            Perhaps one of your companions
            can persuade you to cooperate!

                        WARNECKE
                  (Contemptuously)
            They wouldn't even try!

Slowly Stepan swings his gun to point at Grant and
Steve; Camera pulls back to a WIDER SHOT.

                        STEPAN
            If they are not too elequent now...
            perhaps they will be more persuasive
            - dead!

Warnecke reacts with stunned shock.

                        WARNECKE
            Wait!  You can't!...

                        STEPAN
                  Well?!...

Warnecke doesn't move; slowly Stepan's finger tightens
on the trigger; there is deathly silence in the hut.

168.  QUICK TWO SHOT.  GRANT AND STEVE

      They are looking death in the face.

169.  QUICK C.U. VARNOFF

      He looks excitedly expectant.

170.  QUICK TWO SHOT.  ARIAS AND NITA

      The old man is deadly grave; Nita looks horror-stricken.

171.  QUICK C.U. WARNECKE

      Sweat beads stand out on his forehead; he runs his
      tongue over dry lips.

172.  GROUP SHOT

Suddenly Warnecke breaks.

>               WARNECKE
>       Alright...<u>Alright!</u>...I'll send
>       your message!

>               GRANT
>               (Sharply)
>       Tom.'

>               WARNECKE
>       What's the use, Alan...We've had
>       it...Leave me alone!

He walks over to the radio.

>               WARNECKE
>       I'll need some help...

>               S EPAN
>       Anything you need...

Warnecke opens up the radio - exposing it; he begins
to make connections; Varnoff is covering Grant and
Steve; Stepan is watching Warnecke...

Suddenly the young C.I.A. Agent grabs the radio...and
lifts it high over his head - about to smash it to the
floor...Almost simultaneously Stepan shoots; once -
twice...Nita screams...With super-human effort Warnecke
hurls the radio at the ground...

173.  CLOSE SHOT.  FLOOR.

The radio hits the hard-packed dirt floor - and crashes
into a thousand pieces...

174.  MED. SHOT

Warnecke collapses across the table; Grant and Steve
make a move towards him - but they are checked by
Varnoff's gun; Stepan whirls on them; he is furious.

>               STEPAN
>       The fool!  He has killed all three
>       of you!...

He raises his gun...

>               NITA
>       <u>No</u>!

48.

Startled, Stepan stops; he looks at the girl; Arias
stands at her side.

                    ARIAS
                  (Tightly)
          Gregor!...You cannot kill them
          - like that!...

Stepan geta a contemptuous look on his face; then he
grins unpleasantly.

                    STEPAN
          You are right, Emilio...They may
          serve a better purpose!

He turns to Varnoff, who is watching Nita with a lewd
grin.

                    STEPAN
                  (Sharply)
          Take them away!  Put them in the
          empty tool shop.

Varnoff gun-gestures at Grant and Steve.

                    VARNOFF
          Come on...move!...

They start off; Camera dollies in across them to a
CLOSE TWO SHOT of NITA and ARIAS; the girl looks grave
and tense; Arias has a haunted expression on his face...

                              DISSOLVE

175.  EXT. NIGHT.  MED. L.S.   TOOL SHOP HUT

It is a small but sturdy looking bamboo hut standing
at the edge of the clearing at a little distance from
the bug hut; the single door faces the clearing; before it stands an armed sentry; it is a bright, moon-
lit night.

176.  INT. NIGHT.  TOOL SHOP.  MED. SHOT

Along the heavy bamboo walls are placed long, sturdy
work tables; racks and stands for tools are evident,
but the hut is completely empty; the floor is hard-
packed dirt; two small windows - through which the
moonlight streams into the hut - both open out towards
the clearing; the back wall is windowless, as are
the two side walls.  Steve and Grant are inspecting
the place.

                    STEVE
What do you make of it, Alan?

                    GRANT
Don't know...Only one thing is
certain...We've run into much more
than we bargained for...

                    STEVE
He shot Tom down...like you'd kill
a mosquito!  What kind of man is he?...

                    GRANT
There's nothing here...Might as
well take it easy...wait and see...

The two men sit down on the floor leaning against the
wall.

177.    TWO SHOT

                    STEVE
              (Bitterly)
Gregor Stepan...Colonel Gregor
Stepan...Salesman!...What does he
mean?  What's he got to sell?

                    GRANT
I don't know, Steve...

                    STEVE
Maybe he has found gold...But why
this whole - military set-up?...

                    GRANT
It's more than gold...Got to be...

                    STEVE
But there's nothing of value around
here...certainly nothing worth killing
a man in cold blood for!

                    GRANT
              (Slowly, pensively)
Wait a minute...Perhaps - there is!
To Stepan!..

                    STEVE
              (He looks up)
What?

                    GRANT
One thing...The Canal!

                         STEVE
The Canal!?

                         GRANT
               (With mounting excitement)
Steve - that's it!   The Panama Canal!

                         STEVE
How can Stepan - sell the Canal?...

                         GRANT
He can't...But he can sell the destruc-
tion of the Canal!  What would that
be worth to an enemy of the United States?

                         STEVE
               (Stunned)
Destroy the Canal!...

                         GRANT
               (Urgently)
Listen, Steve...Suppose Stepan has
a way of doing just that...He is
here - in a strategic position - in
complete secrecy - from where he can
strike without warning!  He has a
fabulous prize for sale...The des-
truction of the Panama Canal!

                         STEVE
You think that's why he's here -
with those troops?

                         GRANT
No doubt about it!...It's only seventy
miles to the Canal Zone...World peace
is shaky - he may figure a year - or
two...He is even in a position to
touch it off!

                         STEVE
               (Shaken)
That's - fantastic...

                         GRANT
               (Soberly)
Don't sell Stepan short...One thing
I've learned in the C.I.A....Take
every crackpot seriously - from Hitler
on down!...

                         STEVE
          How can Stepan possibly hope to
          destroy the Canal - even if he has
          a few troops?  It's one of the best
          guarded areas in the world...

                         GRANT
          Remember your history, Steve...How
          did Hannibal defeat the invincible
          Roman legions?  With elephants!  A
          new concept in warfare...Maybe
          Stepan has an elephant of his own...

                         STEVE
          What?...

                         GRANT
                    (Worriedly)
          I don't know,that, Steve...I don't
          know...

178.   INT. NIGHT.  STEPAN'S HUT.  CLOSE OVER SHOULDER SHOT,
       ARIAS TO NITA

       The girl is looking at her father with burning eyes.

                         NITA
                    (Tensely)
          Are you, father?  Are you going
          to do something?  You know what will
          happen...

       Camera pulls out and around to a MED. TWO SHOT.  Arias
       looks deeply troubled and utterly resigned; he ges-
       tures ineffectively with his hands; he avoids the
       girl's eyes.

                         ARIAS
          Nita...Querido...I should not have
          given myself to them...But - what
          else could I do?...

                         NITA
          Father!

                         ARIAS
          When Stepan threatened to harm you,
          Nenita...I had to do what he wanted...
          I - I had to...I...

       He lets the sentence trail away; he lowers his head -
       the picture of a broken dejected man.  Nita gets tears
       in her eyes; she puts her arm around her father.

52.

                    NITA
                  (Gently)
          No es bueno pensar en lo pasada...

Camera dollies in to a CLOSE TWO SHOT.

                    ARIAS
          You are right...It is not good to
          think of what is past...

                    NITA
          I know why you give in to Gregor
          Stepan, father...Your decision - it
          made you do a wrong thing...For that
          you pay in your heart...

                    ARIAS
          (In a dead tone of voice)
          I helped - create - this monstrous
          thing...I, Emilio Manuel Arias...
          But...He had you...He - would have...

He looks confused and defeated.

                    NITA
          Now you must be strong, father.

                    ARIAS
          Strong?  Against a man like Stepan?...

                    NITA
          You must stop him.  You know what he
          will do.  You must stop it!

For a moment Arias looks full at his daughter; then
his head sinks down again.

                    ARIAS
          There is nothing I can do, Nenita...
          Nothing I can do...

Again he makes a small, ineffective gesture with his
hands; Camera dollies in to a C.U. of Nita; tears
well up in her eyes; she regards her father both
with pity and love - and with grief for this broken
shell of a men...

                                        DISSOLVE

179.  INT. NIGHT.  TOOL SHOP HUT.  MED SHOT

Steve and grant are dozing.  Camera slowly dollies in
to a CLOSE SHOT.  All is quiet - except for the jungle

                                        (CONT.)

179.  CONTINUED

night noises...

Suddenly - from outside - there is the sound of a motor
starting up and being gunned and a strange 'whooshing'
sound...

Both Steve and Grant sit up with a start; they look at
each other...The motor noise gets louder - and so do
the angry and alarmed jungle cries answering it...

180.  ANOTHER ANGLE

Steve runs to one of the small windows - Grant follows
him; Steve looks out.

                   STEVE
          Alan!  Look!...
            (He turns to Grant)
        There's _your_ _elephant_!

Both men look out at the clearing; the motor sounds
rise in pitch!

181.  EXT. NIGHT. L.S.  TOOL SHOP HUT P.O.V.

In the clearing, brightly lit by a full moon, several
small groups of men are gathered.  From a spot quite
close to the little hut a tiny, strange looking aircraft is just taking off - soaring into the air...It
is a _one-man_ helicopter - _a_ _rotorcycle_! As Camera
follows it, it climbs rapitly straight up; then it
performs a series of quick, breathtaking maneuvres...

       (NOTE:  The _Rotorcycle_, developed and manufac-
       tured by Hiller Helicopters of Palo Alto, Cali-
       fornia,is the world's smallest and newest air-
       craft...Weighing only 300 pounds it can carry
       one man plus a payload of hundreds of pounds.
       It is completely foldable into a compact pack,
       which can be carried in the back of a station
       wagon, and it can be assembled in the span of
       several minutes.  Ready to fly it looks roughly
       like this:  A compact, three-foot-long engine
       housing with the pilot seat attached; two rotor
       blades on top, and a short tail assembly; and a
       tripod landing gear.  This incredibly small one-
       man helicopter can perform near impossible feats
       of maneuvring, and has obtained a fantastic air
       mobility.  Its size, excellent portability,
       transport capacity, and the fact that it literally
       can land anywhere, makes this new rotorcycle an
       invaluable item in countless military problems,

                            (CONT.)

and it makes it possible for heavily armed assault troops to move into strategic enemy areas many miles away, swiftly - and without warning!)

182. CLOSE TWO SHOT.  HUT WINDOW.  STEVE AND GRANT

The two men are looking out the window; their faces mirror stunned incredulity.

183. THE CLEARING.  ROTORCYCLE MANEUVRES

The rotorcycle maneuvres will be routined in the field to take best advantage of the astounding and exciting performance of this fabulous, tiny helicopter.  As many rotorcycles as can be obtained should be used in this scene, to make it as impressive as possible.  As Grant and Steve are watching, spellbound, one group of two or three men assembles a rotorcycle - and it takes off within minutes...

184. MED. SHOT.  HUT WINDOW.

Steve and Grant are looking out; the Sentry at the door walks past the window; he sees the two men watching; he jabs his rifle butt at the window.

                    SENTRY
                   (Gruffly)
          Get away from there!...

185. INT. NIGHT.  TOOL SHOP HUT.  MED. SHOT

Steve and Grant quickly draw away from the window; outside the Sentry bangs on the wall.

                    SENTRY (O.S.)
          And stay away!

Excited Steve and Grant squat on the bare floor; Camera dollies in to a CLOSE TWO SHOT; from outside the motor noises can be heard faintly through this scene...

                    GRANT
                   (Grimly)
          He can do it, Steve...Stepan
          can destroy the Canal!

                    STEVE
          What are those things?...

                    GRANT
          Rotorcycles...One-man helicopters...
          Stepan's got a force of flying comman-
          dos here...With each carrying one small
          nuclear bomb - they could reach the Gatun
          Dam in less then an hour!

                    STEVE
          What about radar?

                    GRANT
          No good...Those things would
          skim the tree tops...

     Grant turns to look at Steve gravely.

186.   C.U.   GRANT

                    GRANT
          In a lightening, completely
          unexpected raid they'd come
          swarming out of the jungle -
          like deadly hornets...Within
          minutes after the first alarm
          they'd b over their target!

187.   TWO SHOT

                    STEVE
          But - our defenses...They'd be
          shot down...

                    GRANT
          Anti-aircraft fire can't bring
          down aircraft that skip across
          the ground like grasshoppers...

                    STEVE
          Ground fire?...

                    GRANT
          They'd get some...But enough of
          them would make it - and return
          to their hidden base here...
          If ever a crackpot had a foolproof
          plan...this is it!

                    STEVE
          Then - Stepan does have an ace for
          sale...He could cripple our country's
          most vital supply line for years!

                    GRANT
                 (Urgently)
          We've got to get this back to
          Duncan!

                    STEVE
          Maybe we can get to one of the
          natives...

                              (CONT.)

Suddenly - as Steve talks - there is a lull in the
motor noises from outside...

                    STEVE (CONT)
            ...There must be someone...

In the sudden quiet a amall, scraping sound can be
heard from the back wall of the hut; as soon as the
motor sounds die down - it, too, a split second later,
stops...as if dependant on the louder noise for its
existance...

                    STEVE (CONT)
            ...that boy...

Grant takes his arm; he whispers sharply...

                    GRANT
            Quiet!...Listen!...

For a moment both men listen intently; there is no
 sound; then the motors in the clearing start up
again; Grant and Steve hurry to the back wall; they
press their ears to it...And again the scraping noise
is heard...Grant looks at Steve; he nods towards the
window...

188.    WIDER ANGLE

Steve silently runs to the window; cautiously he peeks
out; then he motions to Grant that 'all is well';
Grant turns back to the wall; Steve joins him.

189.    CLOSE TWO SHOT

Grant takes a deep breath; then he softly knocks on
the bamboo wall - three times...

The scraping noise stops at once...There is a pause
filled with suspense and silence; the two men look
at each other.

                    STEVE
                  (Whispering)
            Some - animal?...

Grant shrugs his shoulders...and them - all at once -
there are three soft taps on the wall from outside!
The men look excited; again Grant taps - and the
scraping noise continues...And suddenly the sharp
point of a machete breaks through the wall into the
hut between two bamboo poles; at once it starts to

                              (CONT)

189.  CONTINUED

saw at the fibre-rope holding the poles together at
intervals...

                          GRANT
              Steve...Do what you can to help
              ...I'll keep a lookout...

                          STEVE
              Right...

Grant hurries away; Steve looks in his pockets; he
finds a lighter, which he returns, and a handkerchief;
he folds the handkerchief; lays it over the exposed
machete blade - and begins to help saw through the
ropes...

190.  CLOSE SHOT.  GRANT

He is cautiously keeping watch at the little window;
the motor noises from outside can be heard - and so
can the sounds of the work on the wall...

191.  CLOSE SHOT.  STEVE

Several of the rope ties have already been cut through..

192.  CLOSE SHOT.  GRANT

He is listening; mingled with the other noises footsteps can be heard approaching outside; Grant stiffens..

193.  WIDER ANGLE

Grant motions to Steve; Steve stops the sawing at once -
and  pushes the machete blade out; then he leans against
the wall as if dozing; Grant stands next to the window,
his back pressed against the wall; the footsteps stop
just outside...

                          VOICE (O.S.)
              Hvor laenge skal du staa vagt?

                          SENTRY (O.S.)
              To timer endnu...

                          VOICE (O.S.)
              Kom saa over og spil et slag kort...

                          SENTRY (O.S.)
              Ja - det skal jeg...

The footsteps start away again; Grant relaxes.

194. CLOSE SHOT. STEVE

Steve taps on the wall; the machete blade re-appears
- and the sawing begins once more...Camera dollies
in to a CLOSE SHOT of the WALL: the sharp machete is
making quick work of the vine-ropes...

DISSOLVE

195. INT. NIGHT. TOOL SHOP HUT. CLOSE SHOT. WALL

Outside the motor noises can still be heard; on the
wall near the floor a square area - large enough for
a man - has been cut through; as we watch the machete
bites through the last bamboo pole...

Camera widens to see Steve and Grant both crouched
before the wall; they carefully push at the cut square..
all at once it gives away - and falls outward...There
is now a hole in the wall...The two men look at it;
in the dim light a face appears...It is Nita!

                    STEVE
                 (Startled)
        Nita!...

                    GRANT
                 (Surprised)
        It's the girl!...

                    NITA
                 (Urgently)
        You must be very quiet...very
        careful...come...

                    GRANT
        What about Stepan?  The others?

                    NITA
        They are busy.  Night nameuvres.
        They always fly at during the dark.

Her face disappears from the opening.

196. WIDER ANGLE

Steve starts for the hole; Grant stops him; he listens
- then he softly goes to the door - and listens again;
he motions for Steve to crawl through the hole; Steve
bends down - and begins to belly through...

197. SHOT. GROUND. STEVE'S P.O.V.

All that can be seen is a close shot of the ground as
Steve slowly pushes through the opening to the outside

(CONT.)

197.   CONTINUED

...The moonlight makes the ground outside appear much
brighter; Steve turns his head slightly...and a pair
of big, black boots comes into view - firmly planted
a little apart!  As Steve's field of view quickly
widens, he sees two more pair of booted legs - and the
slim legs of Nita...

198.   EXT. NIGHT. BACK OF TOOL SHOP HUT.  MED WIDE SHOT

Steve is just getting out of the hole in the wall;
facing him stand Stepan and another soldier, Dietrich,
a ram-rod, cold man in his thirties; next to them
stands Varnoff, holding Nita in a firm grip - his hand
clamped over her mouth tightly; he is obviously
enjoying his task...

                    STEPAN
               (With cold sarcasm)
          Good evening, Mr. Carter!  Are
          you going somewhere?!...

Steve stands up; Grant follows him out through the hole;
they are facing the guns in the hands of Stepan and
Dietrich; Varnoff takes his hand from Nita's mouth -
but he keeps on holding her, during:

                    STEPAN
          I must congratulate you, gentlemen!
          Your charm must be quite considerable
          to have persuaded little Nita to take
          this drastic and foolhardy step on
          such short acquaintance!

Varnoff scowls at Steve and Grant; Stepan glares at him.

                    STEPAN
          Varnoff!  Let the girl go!  She
          will join her friends...

Reluctantly Varnoff lets Nita go; she at once steps
away from him...

                    STEPAN
               (Sarcastic)
          Unfortunately I'm afraid I must
          spoil your project...You see,
          the Indians need another example
          set; they are getting a little
          out of hand...I have no doubt that
          you - the three of you - will provide
          my more rebellious native elements
          with a perfect object lesson!

He turns to Dietrich.

> STEPAN
> (Curtly)
> Alright, Dietrich...To the cave!...

They start off...

199.  EXT. NIGHT. L.S. NATIVE VILLAGE

Several huts made of bamboo and leaves, some of them on
stilts, make up the village.  It is deserted; the stilt
huts look dead - and ominously watchful at the same
time; through the village walks a little procession:
First Dietrich; then Steve and Grant with Nita; then
Stepan and Varnoff; only now and again a straw mat is
quickly drawn tighter over a hut entrance as the party
passes by- out of sight...

200.  EXT. NIGHT. L.S. CAVE MOUTH

It is the mouth of a large cave in the mountainside;
in front of it is a small clearing; an armed soldier
stands guard at the cave entrance; it is Zabala, a
Latin American; off to the left through the jungle
can be seen several tents, the camp of Stepan's men;
at the cave entrance a small fire is burning...The
Party comes up to the cave mouth and stops.

201.  CLOSER GROUP SHOT.

Stepan addressed the guard.

> STEPAN
> Zabala.  Get a torch.

Zabala picks up a torch; lights it in the fire...

> STEPAN
> Go ahead...

They start into the cave...Stepan in the lead with
Zabala.

202.  INT. CAVE.  MED. L.S.

It is a large natural cave; along one wall several
small boxes and crates are stored; the cave goes on back
deep into the mountain - and it is apparent, even in
the limited light from the torch, that stretching on
into the cave are row upon row of large crates, each
containing a compactly folded rotorcycle!  A couple
of the little aircraft - partly assembled - stand off
by themselves; a small side tunnel is blocked off and
bears a warning sign in four languages:

(CONT.)

Spanish, German, Russian and English...

                    WARNING - DANGER!

The men come to a place, where the cave widens out a
little; and suddenly - in the flickering light from
the torch - two figures can be seen lying on the floor
against the wall; they are both natives; one is a
handsome man in his thirties, with proud but angry
eyes; the other is the young boy, Eneepe; they are both
tied hand and foot...Stepan stops.

                    STEPAN
          Ah!  Here we are!
            (He turns to Steve and Grant)
          May I present the Chief of this
          tribe, Sagala Coman...and his son,
          Eneepe, whom you have already met!

Dietrich lights another torch set in the wall, during:

                    STEPAN
          Coman and I do not see eye to eye on
          some things...But as long as he remains
          my - eh - guest...his people behave..!

He turns abruptly to his men.

                    STEPAN
          Tie them up!

Dietrich and Varnoff go towards a rock outcropping on
the wall; several lengths of rope are hanging across
the rock; they each take off a length...

                                        DISSOLVE

203.  INT. CAVE.  CLOSE SHOT ROCK OUTCROPPING

      Almost all of the rope is gone; Camera dollies out and
      pans to see Steve, Grant and Nita lying on the ground,
      tied hand and foot; Coman and Eneepe lie nearby;  The
      cave is illuminated by the torch on the wall.

                    GRANT
              (Straining against his
               bonds)
          No use...Can't get loose...

      Steve turns to Nita.

                    STEVE
          I'm sorry we got you into this...

                    NITA
          (With suppressed vehemence)
          I wish you had never come!

Steve and Grant look at each other in surprise; Coman
has been listening intently; there is no sound from the
cave entrance; he turns to Eneepe.

                    COMAN
          (In a sharp whisper)
          Eneepe.  Use your teeth!

Quietly, like two big snakes, the Indians wriggle towards each other; Coman turns so his bound hands are
held towards his son.  Eneepe silently positions himself so he can reach the rope around his father's
wrists with his teeth; doggedly he begins to try to
get a hold.

204.  CLOSE THREE SHOT.  STEVE, GRANT AND NITA.

They are watching; hope seems to revive in Nita's eyes;
Steve and Grant remain silent - only glance at each
other, then watch the natives eagerly.

205.  CLOSE SHOT

The ropes around Coman's hands are tight, cutting into
the flesh of his wrists.  Eneepe can find no hold with
his teeth.

206.  MED. SHOT

Coman is aware of Eneepe's trouble.

                    COMAN
          You must bite through!

Eneepe briefly raises his head.

                    ENEEPE
          (Seriously)
          Yes, father...

Eneepe returns to his task; the others watch anxiously.

207.  CLOSE SHOT

Eneepe's sharp teeth gnaw at the taut rope; he cannot
get hold without also biting into his father's skin;
a small trickle of blood runs down Coman's wrists;
Eneepe stops gnawing.

208. C.U. COMAN

                    COMAN
        Do not stop!

209. MED. SHOT. ANOTHER ANGLE

                   ENEEPE
      But - I am hurting you, father!...

                   COMAN
               (Sharply)
     Obey me, Eneepe!  Use your teeth

Eneepe resumes biting and gnawing; again and again his
sharp teeth penetrate his father's skin.

210. C.U. COMAN

His face is stony, expressionless; the muscles in his
jaws stand out as he clamps his teeth together.

211. GROUP SHOT

Steve turns to Nita.

                   STEVE
     Nita...How many men does Stepan
     have?

The girl remains sullen and silent.

                   GRANT
              (Sternly)
     Look, Nita...Whatever your reasons
     - you're one of us now...You must
     help us - if we are to get out of
     this...Now answer the question!

Slowly the girl turns towards the two men.

                   NITA
     Stepan has more than one hundred men.

Grant whistles softly.

                   STEVE
     How on earth did he get here...?  How
     did he get all that equipment - all
     his supplies - those torotcycles -
     in here?...

                         NITA
          They were put ashore -many months
          ago - by submarine, at night...on a
          Lonely coast...They made their way
          through the jungle...

                         GRANT
          So that's why they weren't detected...

     There is the sudden sound of a small sob from the
     direction of Coman and Eneepe; the three of them look
     toward the two Indians...

212.  CLOSE SHOT

          Eneepe is tenaciously chewing on the tough rope; he
          gives a small sob; his mouth is smeared with the blood
          from his father's wounds; he has tears in his eyes.
          CAMERA PANS from Eneepe to a CLOSE SHOT of the torch
          burning brightly...The flames leap in a merry dance...

                                        DISSOLVE

213.  INT. NIGHT. STEPAN'S HUT.  CLOSE SHOT.  MILITARY MAKE
      KEROSENE LAMP

          It is burning brightly - hanging from the ceiling over
          the table; Camera pulls out and down to a MED SHOT.
          Stepan and Varnoff are sitting at the table; two or
          three rifles are lying at one end of it with a couple
          of telescopic sights, ahich Varnoff is finishing
          cleaning; a bottle of Vodka stands on the floor beside
          him; occasionally he takes a drink; a stack of maps
          and documents lies before Stepan, who is working on
          them at the opposite end of the table;  a small
          document or map case also can be seen.  Varnoff spits
          on a piece of cloth and polishes a telescopic sight
          lens with loving care...

                         VARNOFF
          How's he taking it...
             (He nods towards the back
             door)
          The old man?...

                         STEPAN
             (Contemptuously)
          Arias?  He does what I say!

     Varnoff takes a drink from his bottle.

                         VARNOFF
          He is very fond of his little
          Nita!

65.

                         STEPAN
                Dietrich is keeping an eye on
                him...I almost wish he would
                try something...

He grins unpleasantly.

214.  WIDER ANGLE

Varnoff gets up; he puts away the gun and sights, during:

                         VARNOFF
                He won't...

Stepan puts some of the documents in the map case -
and Varnoff takes a drink, during:

                         VARNOFF
                What about those Americans?  What
                really brought them here?...

                         STEPAN
                     (Frowning)
                I am not sure...After tomorrow it
                will not matter...

                         VARNOFF
                There may be others...

                         STEPAN
                Perhaps...and that is why...
                     (Resolutely)
                I have decided to play for an
                early D-Day!

Varnoff reacts.

                         VARNOFF
                There may not be an opportunity...

                         STEPAN
                I'll make my own opportunity!  I
                am sending orders for our man in
                Panama to make contact - at once!

                         VARNOFF
                Good...

215.  M.C.U.  STEPAN

He grabs documents and maps from the stack before him
as emphasis as he talks.

                         (CONT.)

                    STEPAN
          Here it is!  The greatest coup in
          the world...Every detail...Nothing
          overlooked...Nothing left to chance...
          Air Patrol Schedules...Stress points
          on the dam...Battery placements...
          maps...A fortune in the palm of my
          hand!...we can't fail!

Stepan puts the rest of the documents and maps in the
document case and hands it to Varnoff...Camera widens
to show action...

                    STEPAN
          Here...Take this to the Staff tent
          ...I will meet with all officers
          tomorrow - after we have taken care
          of our visitors...

Varnoff takes the document case.

                    VARNOFF
          Yes, Colonel...

Stepan settles back in his chair; Camera dollies in to
a tight C.U. as Stepan lights up a cigar...He leans
back in his chair and regards the burning match with
an expression of cruel satisfaction...

                              DISSOLVE

216.  CLOSE SHOT.  THE TORCH

      The torch has almost burned out.  Camera pans to a
      CLOSE GROUP SHOT. Suddenly Coman grunts; with a
      savage wrench he rips apart the last shreds  of the
      cords binding his hands.  Immediately he sits up and
      holds his hands in front of him.

217.  CLOSE SHOT.  COMAN'S HANDS

      Coman's left wrist bears two ugly wounds, where Eneepe's
       teeth have bitten into his skin.  The cuts bleed
      freely; Coman flexes his fingers.

218.  MED. SHOT

      Coman quickly unties his feet, and frees Eneepe.
      Silently the two Indians stand up.

219.  CLOSE TWO SHOT.  COMAN AND ENEEPE

      They listen intently; there is no sound.

220. CLOSE THREE SHOT.  STEVE, GRANT AND NITA

They are watching expectantly.

221. MED. SHOT.  DIFFERENT ANGLE

Silently, stealthily Coman begins to move towards the tunnel cave entrance - ignoring the three other captives completely.  Eneepe places his hand on his father's arm - stopping him.

222. CLOSE TWO SHOT.  COMAN AND ENEEPE

Eneepe looks towards the girl and the two Americans, still lying bound on the floor; then he gives his father an inquiring look.

                    COMAN
          They are white!  Bad!  Like all!

Eneepe keeps looking at Coman - earnestly...

223. MED. SHOT.  ACROSS STEVE, GRANT AND NITA TO COMAN
     AND ENEEPE.

Without a word Coman quickly and silently turns back; it is only a moment's work, and Steve, Grant and Nita are free too.  Eneepe is watching and listening at the tunnel entrance to the cave.

                    STEVE
               (Rubbing his wrists)
          Thank you, Coman...

                    COMAN
               (He sucks his wounds;
                coldly)
          My son is right. You are in my
          village.  My charge.  You go with
          me.

Nita solicitously moves up to Coman; she reaches for his injured wrist.

                    NITA
          Here...Let me look at that...

Coman pulls his arm away angrily.

                    COMAN
               No!

He turns abruptly to leave.

                    STEVE
          Wait!

Coman stops; Steve walks up to him followed by Grant.

224.   THREE SHOT

                    STEVE
          We must have a plan, Coman...Where
          do we go?  How?

                    COMAN
          To the big water...find fishing
          village...

                    STEVE
          How far?

                    COMAN
          Six days!  Through jungle.  I
          know...

                    GRANT
          Six days!  We'll need weapons -
          food...

Coman looks quickly at Grant;  He thinks rapidly.

                    COMAN
          Men-that-fly sleep.  We take
          guns - food...

225.   MED. SHOT

                    GRANT
           We'll need a good headstart...
          Once Stepan discovers we've gone,
          he'll follow...He'll have to try
          to catch us...or...
               (He turns to Coman)
          Is there no place nearer we can
          get help?

Coman shakes his head.

                    GRANT
          Alright...The coast, then...We...

He is interrupted as Eneepe suddenly comes running
up to them; he makes a sigh of silence.  They all
listen breathlessly.  Faint voices can be heard from
just outside the cave.

     ZABALA (O.S.)
   Meeting over, Varnoff?

      VARNOFF (O.S.)
   <u>Da</u> - for now.  You take a break...
   I will stand guard for you a little
   while...

      ZABALA (O.S.)
    (Insinuation in his voice)
   See your chance at last?!...She is
   not bad, that Nita...

      VARNOFF (O.S.)
    (He gives a short bark of
     laughter)
   Waited long time!  Now - take
   off!...

From the tunnel entrance comes the sound of heavy,
unsteady footsteps, crunching on the gravel...

Quickly the four captives fall to the ground - their
hands behind them, as if they were still trussed up;
in the dim light of the cave it is difficult to see
distinctly.  Almost as soon as they are down, a man
steps into view in the cave.

226. CLOSE SHOT

The man stands near the wall; he is lurching silently;
it is Varnoff; he has a gun in his belt, and the small
document case slung over his shoulder.

227. MED. SHOT.  ANOTHER ANGLE

Varnoff slowly walks over to where Nita lies on the
ground; he leers down at her.  His big, hammy fists
are twitching in excitement and ill suppressed desire.

      VARNOFF
   You are not very comfortable,
   little one...not happy...

228. C. U.  VARNOFF

He wipes the back of his hand across wet lips; he
stares sensuously at Nita.

      VARNOFF
   Varnoff like you...all the time...
   Perhaps you be nice to him now - if
   he helps you...Yes?...

229. MED. SHOT

Varnoff bends down to untie Nita's legs. Suddenly
Steve leaps up - immediately followed by Grant, Coman
and Eneepe. Steve deals the startled, drunken Varnoff
a savage rabbit blow across the neck - but he is not
quite quick enough; the brute lets out a roar of
enraged surprise before other blows from Steve and
Grant send him crashing to the cave floor - uncon-
scious...

230. INT. STEPAN'S HUT. M.C.U.

Stepan is lying in his hammock only half dressed under
his mosquito net; next to his head stands a rifle,
leaning against the wall; the telescopic sight is off,
lying on a box nearby. Stepan sits up with a start...

231. INT. CAVE. MED. SHOT

The little group is on its feet - staring at the felled
Varnoff; faintly - distantly from the outside can be
heard Stepan's voice bellowing:

                    STEPAN (O.S.)
          Varnoff!...

There is the sudden, sharp report of a rifle shot,
which echoes through the jungle. The people in the
cave are startled into action.

                    GRANT
          Quick! Let's get out of here -
          the camp's alerted...

                    STEVE
          The weapons - food...

                    GRANT
          No time. Grab what you can find...

Grant himself takes the gun from Varnoff's belt; Steve
grabs the document case; quickly they all run to the
cave mouth.

232. MED. SHOT. INT. CAVE MOUTH

It is dawn outside; the little group comes running up
to the cave entrance; cautiously Grant looks out, then
quickly turn to Coman.

                    GRANT
          Coman! The jungle...We'll follow...

Swiftly Coman and Eneepe run past the white people to
the cave mouth; Coman quickly surveys the area outside...

233.  CLOSE SHOT.  STEVE

He is standing near a ledge on the cave wall.  On it
a few cooking utensils, pots, bowls and baskets, are
placed - also a small _knife_, which Steve grabs.

234.  MED. SHOT.  INT. CAVE MOUTH

Coman turns to the others.

                    COMAN
          Must run quick!  Come!...

He begins to run out; the others follow him.  Eneepe
has spied a pile of sleeping mats stacked near the
entrance; on top of it lies a child's toy; the boy
bends to pick it up...

235.  CLOSE SHOT.  ENEEPE

He is grabbing the toy on the run; it is a small
_blowgun_ with a handful of little _darts_.

236.  EXT. DAWN. L.S. VILLAGE

The cave entrance can be seen in the B.G.  The five
fugitives come running from the cave and head for
the village and the jungle beyond.

237.  ANOTHER ANGLE.  L.S.

The fugitives come running through the village; in
the B.G. a couple of soldiers come into view; they fire
at the running escapees...Suddenly - unnoticed by the
five - to the side and a little in front of them a man
appears - gun in hand...He stops short as he sees the
running figures...It is Arias!

238.  QUICK SHOT.  MED. CLOSE SHOT, ARIAS

He stands in indecision.

239.  L.S.

Suddenly another man joins Arias; it is Dietrich; at
once the newcomer raises his gun to shoot...

240.  ANGLE.  ACROSS DIETRICH AND ARIAS TO RUNNING FUGITIVES

The fleeing five have seen Dietrich and Arias now;

73.

dismayed they veer off their straight course for the
jungle.  Suddenly Arias gets a determined look on his
face; he springs into action - and knocks Dietrich's
gun into the air - just as he fires...The two men
grabble for the gun...

241.  TWO SHOT.  DIETRICH AND ARIAS

They are struggling for the gun; there is a sudden
report - and Arias draws up in agony; he turns to
look in the direction from where the shot came...

242.  MED. L.S. ARIAS' P.O.V.

It is Stepan; he looks furious; he is running towards
Dietrich and Arias; he stops and raises his gun, aiming towards the fugitives...

243.  ANGLE ACROSS DIETRICH AND ARIAS TO FUGITIVES

Arias pitches to the ground - dead; in the B.G. Nita
has seen her father shot; she stops ; Steve and Grant
turn to bring her along...

244.  THREE SHOT.  NITA, STEVE AND GRANT

Nita looks horrified; a bullet whizzes by them.

                    NITA
          Father!

                    STEVE
               (Taking her arm)
          You can't help him now...Come
          on!...

Grant has turned towards the pursuers; eh shoots once -
twice - with Varnoff's gun; then he follows Steve and
Nita - who have again started for the nearby jungle...
(Intercut= 244a = One or two of Stepan's men are hit
by Grant)

245.  MED. SHOT.  STEPAN

He raises his rifle and aims.

                    STEPAN
               (Shouting)
          Get them!...

246.  SHOT ACROSS STEPAN'S RIFLE TO THE FUGITIVES IN THE B.G.

Stepan's gun roars and belches flame; in the B.G.
Grant stumbles and falls to the ground.

247.  CLOSER ANGLE.  GRANT

Grant tries to get up; he can't; Steve and Nita have
reached the jungle edge; at once Steve turns and runs
to Grant; he takes hold of him and drags him the last
few steps to the jungle.

248.  THREE SHOT.  STEVE, GRANT AND NITA

Grant sinks to the ground at the edge of the jungle
clearing; Steve and Nita crouch anxiously over him...

                    GRANT
                 (Urgently)
          Get out of here, Steve...Get back
          to Duncan...

                    STEVE
          We can't leave you...

                    GRANT
          Do as I say!

                    STEVE
          But...

                    GRANT
          Damn it!  We are not important!
          But what we know is!  I've got
          a couple of rounds left...I'll hold
          them off as long as I can...

He turns around to face the village clearing; the gun
is held out before him; Steve grabs his shoulder...

                    STEVE
          So long...Alan!...

Quickly he turns and runs off into the jungle with
Nita.

249.  EXT. DAWN. L.S.  JUNGLE CLEARING  (SAME AS LOCATION
WHERE JUAN WAS KILLED)

Steve and Nita are running across the little clearing;
they are almost across, when Nita stumbles and falls;
Steve bends to help her up...

250.  TWO SHOT

                    STEVE
          We'll have to reach the coast
          without Coman...Think you can
          make it?

Nita is getting up; her face is tear-streaked; she
merely nods; they start off.

251. MED. SHOT

They are nearing the jungle edge; suddenly two figures
step out into view; Steve and Nita stop in shock -
then they recognize Coman and Eneepe; Coman beckons -
and the four of them run off quickly to disappear into
the jungle...

252. EXT. DAWN. JUNGLE EDGE OF VILLAGE CLEARING. SHOT ACROSS
GRANT LYING HIDDEN IN F.G. TO STEPAN, DIETRICH AND
ZABALA

Grant lies absolutely still; in his hand held out before
him is Varnoff's gun - pointed straight at the men
running towards him...

Closer and closer they come - until they are almost on
top of him...(build for suspense)  Suddenly Stepan
sees Grant; in startled fear he stops - and jumps back;
Grant makes no move; then - curiously - Stepan walks
over to the man lying on the ground; he looks down at
him - and turns him over with his boot; Zabala and
Dietrich join him...

                    STEPAN
          One down...Four to go...!

He bends down and removes the gun from Grant's hand;
there is a noise in the distance in the jungle;
nervously Zabala and Dietrich fire into the thicket;
Stepan stops them with a sharp command. (Note=
Alternate possibility: Regular gun fight in which
Grant is killed - but none of the main enemies.)

                    STEPAN
          Zabala!  Dietrich!  Wait...

253. M.C.U.  STEPAN

                    STEPAN
          Let them go!  Don't waste your
          bullets.  We'll get them another
          way.

He grins in cold anticipation.

254. MED. L.S.

The men start back towards the village; in the B.G.

                              (CONT.)

Varnoff comes staggering from the cave, holding his
head in his hands; he shakes it - and stumbles towards
the others.  Diego, Jose and other of Stepan's men and
native crew come running from the far camp.

> STEPAN
> Get plenty of ammunition.  Put
> the scopes on your rifles...
> (He grins mirthlessly)
> ...We're going hunting!

> DIETRICH
> We can use the rotorcycles!

> STEPAN
> No.  Jungle is too dense.  We'd
> never see them...

Diego joins the group; he is a small man, part Spanish
part Indian; he is in charge of Stepan's native workers;
Stepan turns to him.

> STEPAN
> Get your boys ready, Diego...Fill
> the canteens.  We must be ready to
> move out within the half-hour.
> Move!

Diego takes off.

255.  MED. SHOT

> ZABALA
> (Nervously; impatiently)
> Why don't we go after them right
> now?

> STEPAN
> (Coldly; calculating)
> The better a hunting safari is
> organized - the better the chance
> of bringing back the game.

> DIETRICH
> They're getting a good headstart...

> STEPAN
> They've got six days to go to reach
> a settlement - no matter which direc-
> tion they take...We'll have them
> before the day is over.  Now - let's
> go!

>                    ZABALA
>                (Wetting his lips)
>            Suppose they do get away?!...

>                    STEPAN
>                  (Mockingly)
>            Four unarmed runaways - against
>            experienced hunters with high-
>            powered rifles?

>                    ZABALA
>            We've got to get them...

>                    STEPAN
>            We will!  And when we do - we
>            won't take any chances.

Varnoff joins the group; he looks slightly dazed;
Stepan turns to him.

>                    STEPAN
>                  (Sharply)
>            What happened?

>                    VARNOFF
>            They were loose...They jumped me...

Suddenly he reaches in horror for the document case.

>                    VARNOFF
>            The document case!...They took it!

256.  C.U. ZABALA

He reacts.

257.  M.C.U.  STEPAN

His eyes are mere slits.

>                    STEPAN
>                (He spits the word)
>            Idiot!

258.  MED. SHOT

>                    STEPAN
>            Get going!

The men all hurriedly disperse, except Stepan.  Camera
moves in to a C.U. as Stepan looks towards the awaken-
ing jungle; he smiles a grim smile of anticipation;
then abruptly he turns and hurries off.

259.    EXT. DAY.  A JUNGLE PATH.  MED. SHOT

Steve and Nita are running along the path; ahead of
them run Coman and Eneepe.  Nita trips and almost
falls; Steve catches her, but she sinks down on the
ground, exhausted.

                    NITA
          Just - let me catch my breath...
          please...

Steve sinks down beside her; he glances back anxiously;
there is not a sound.  Ahead of them Coman and Eneepe
have stopped too; silently they are waiting.

                    STEVE
          It's alright.  You're doing fine.
          We should be quite a bit ahead of
          them...

260.    TWO SHOT.

                    NITA
              (Tears well up in her eyes)
          They killed him...They killed my
          father...

                    STEVE
          He gave us our chance, Nita...

                    NITA
              (With bitter resentment)
          All because of you!  Why did you
          have to come?!...

                    STEVE
          If you resented us so much - why
          did you try to help us?

Nita looks at him darkly for a moment.

                    NITA
          I do not want your blood on
          my father's hands...

                    STEVE
              (He is silent for a moment)
          Why - why was your father part of
          - this...?

                    NITA
              (Bitterly)
          Because of me.

                         STEVE
          You!?

                         NITA
          Stepan - threatened to kill me,
          if father did not help...

                         STEVE
          Why your father?

                         NITA
          Father knew this area better than
          anyone...As a mining engineer...
          he guided Stepan to Coman's village -
          helped with the natives in the beginn-
          ing...He was afraid to seek help from
          anyone - because of me...

                         STEVE
          I see...

                         NITA
           (With tears in her eyes)
          It made him a broken man...He was
          weak - without courage...
           (She looks up at Steve;
            defiantly)
          But he was alive!...And I was with
          him...
                 (Eyes blazing)
          Then you had to come!

                         STEVE
                 (Gently)
          And your father got back his courage...
          his self respect...He became a man again!

          Nita's head sinks down...

                         STEVE (CONT.)
          He gave his life for us, Nita...
          For you.

          Nita looks up at Steve in serious thoughtfulness; then
          she glances back into the junble.

                         NITA
          I - I haven't heard anything at
          all.  Are they following us?

                         STEVE
                 (Grimly)
          You can be sure of that!  They'll
          be hunting us down...

                         NITA
                      (Quietly)
            We don't have much of a chance,
            do we?


                         STEVE
            If only we could fight back...
                  (He looks with frustration
                    at his little woman's knife)
            But all I've got is a woman's knife...
                  (He nods towards the two
                    Indians squatting on the
                    trail ahead)
            ...And they, a toy - a child's
            blowgun!


                         NITA
                  (Looking towards Coman
                    and Eneepe)
            I wonder why they haven't left
            us - they could do so much better
            alone...


                         STEVE
                      (Thoughtfully)
            ...They have a strict code of
            honor...Let's be grateful they're
            still with us...

261.   MED. SHOT.   STEVE AND NITA IN F.G.   COMAN AND ENEEPE
       IN B.G.

                         STEVE
            Coman knows the jungle - we wouldn't
            have a chance without him...
                  (he looks speculatively
                    at Coman)
            Perhaps he knows that...

Suddenly there is a couple of sharp yelps - like a dog
barking - not too far away.  Steve and Nita jump up;
they run to Coman.

                         STEVE
            Coman!  Dogs!  They're tracking us
            with dogs!...

                         COMAN
            Yeeno...Wild dog.  No men yet...

He turns to resume the flight.

                          COMAN
                   We go on now...

They all run down the path.

262.  EXT. DAY.  VILLAGE.  EDGE OF JUNGLE.

Stepan, Zabala, Dietrich, Varnoff and Diego are gathered
at the jungle edge where the four fugitives disappeared
into the thicket.  The men - with the exception of
Diego - all carry their highpowered rifles, telescopic
sights in place; Diego carries a long machete with a
broad blade.  Each man also had a small knapsack on
his back and a belt to hold extra ammunition and a
canteen.  Jose and three native cargadores, loaded with
their burdens, stand nearby, ready to follow the hunters

                          STEPAN
                   (Patting his rifle)
                   Alright, let's go!
                   (To Diego)
                   Diego!  You do the tracking. See
                   that you don't loose their trail!

                          DIEGO
                   Si, Coronel!  I track!

Eagerly Diego turns and at a half-trot enters the
thick jungle; the others follow him in single file.

263.  EXT. DAY.  L.S.  JUNGLE PATH

Coman, Nita, Steve and Eneepe, in that order, are
running along the narrow path; Coman in the lead is
a bit in front of Nita.  They all pass Camera in M.C.U's.

264.  MED. SHOT.  THE PATH

The four fugitives are running along the trail.

265.  C.U. STEVE.  TRAVEL SHOT

He looks back; concerned.

266.  C.U. NITA.  TRAVEL SHOT

She looks winded and frightened.

267.  MED. SHOT.  NITA'S P.O.V.  RUNNING SHOT (EYEMO)

Coman is running easily with a loping gait in front
of Nita (Camera); he comes to a place where a wild
boar trail crosses the path; he continues on.  Nita
(Camera) nears the same place; a thick - heavily
foliaged branch stretch out over the path.  Suddenly

                                        (CONT.)

267.  CONTINUED

a gigantic python snake partly falls from the branch
to hang suspended - hissing malevolently - a mere foot
in front of Nita's face; she stops short...

268.  C.U.  NITA

She screams in terror.

269.  MED. SHOT.  PATH AND TRAIL CROSSING

Panic-stricken Nita whirls away from the huge serpent
and darts down the wild boar trail.  Coman has turned,
when Nita screamed; as he sees her race down the wild
boar trail he shouts with unsuspected power and author-
ity:

                    COMAN
          Stop!

270.  C.U. COMAN - OVERLAPPING

                    COMAN
          Wedera!

271.  MED. SHOT. WILD BOAR TRAIL.  ACROSS NITA FACING
CAMERA IN F.G. TO TRAIL IN B.G.

Nita stops in her tracks; she puts her hands to her
face, sobbing; and stands  trembling.  Steve runs
quickly to her side from behind her; Coman comes up
to them, followed by Eneepe.

                    STEVE
                  (To Coman)
          What is it?

Without a word Coman runs past Nita and Steve a few
feet along the trail;  Carefully he bends down to
the ground; he shifts a couple of branches and leaves
- and a gaping, black hole lies exposed before them!

Nita shudders and turns to Steve, but she is regaining
her self-control.

                    COMAN
          Wedera! Trap for wild boar...
          This his trail...

Coman at once begins to run back to the path.

                              (CONT.)

                         STEVE
               Wait!...

Coman stops; comes back.

                         STEVE
                        (eagerly)
               How much time do you think we
               have, Coman?  How far are we
               ahead?

                         COMAN
                    (He is not friendly)
               Not far.  Half hour - maybe.  They
               faster then we - get closer all time.

                         STEVE
               Exactly...That trap...If it can
               catch a pig - Why not a man?!

                         COMAN
               Not very deep.  Others get him
               out quick.

                         STEVE
               But not much good to them - if he's
               disabled!

                         NITA
               Steve...It might work...I've seen
               traps like that...They have sharpened
               sticks at the bottom...Pointed up...

                         ENEEPE
                    (Pointing to the trap.)
               No sticks.  Need pigs alive.

                         NITA
                        (Doubtfully)
               We could put some in...

                         STEVE
               All we have is this ridiculous little
               knife...Would take us ages..and We've only
               got minutes...I have a better idea...
                        (He turns to Coman)
               Coman, that big python...Can we catch it?

Coman's eyes light up.

                         COMAN
               My son and me catch him quick!
                    (He looks with grudging res-
                     pect at Steve)
               You fix plenty good trap!

272. BOAR TRAP AREA.  DIFFERENT SHOTS

Nita sinks down to rest; the three men fly into action;
Eneepe cuts a long length of pliable rattan vine;
Coman - helped by steve, whom he gives short directions
- prepares a long branch for the 'snake stick', he
will use; it is a forked stick with the long rattan
vine made into a draw-loop at the fork end.  The Three
are busy making the 'snake stick'...

DISSOLVE

273. EXT. DAY.  JUNGLE.  BOAR TRAP AREA.  MED. SHOT

The snake-stick is finished; the three men run back to
the path carrying it...

274. MED. SHOT.  PATH AND TRAIL CROSSING

The huge python snake is still hanging from the heavy
branch; it is deadly motionless; regarding the men with
cold, staring eyes...Carefully Coman walks up to the
reptile; a quick motion - and the noose slips over
the serpent's head; Coman pulls the loop - and the
snake is captured.  It takes the full strength of all
three men to get the almost 30-foot-long python off
the branch.

275. MED. SHOT.  WILD BOAR TRAIL.  TRAP

The three men struggle up to the trap and manage to
throw the snake down into the hole.  Coman and Eneepe
cover the trap carefully; Steve helps Nita to her
feet; she looks in horror at the now indistinguishable
trap.

276. TWO SHOT.  STEVE AND NITA

                    NITA
                (Shuddering)
        It's - horrible...

                    STEVE
        I only hope it works...
            (He looks seriously at
              the girl)
        Nita - you do understand...It's -
        It's their lives...or ours!

                    NITA
        I know...

277.   MED. SHOT.   ANOTHER ANGLE

                    COMAN
          Men come near.  We go...

Coman and Eneepe begin to run ahead on the wild boar
trail.

                    STEVE
          Right...
                    (To Nita)
          Go ahead...I'll be with you in
          a second.

Nita starts off - looking back for Steve; Steve rips
off a small piece of his shirt sleve, fastens it in
plain view on a bush on the far side of the trap, and
runs after the others.  With Coman in the lead they
cut  off the boar trail and circle back towards the
path.  Camera holds until they are out of sight.

278.   EXT. DAY. L.S. JUNGLE PATH

The hunters come running down the path; they use the
fast, enduring half-trot of the experienced tracker.
With the exception of Diego each man carries his
rifle with telescopic sight; Diego carries his machete;
he is in the lead, tracking, closely followed by
Stepan, Zabala, Dietrich and Varnoff; the cargadores
bring up the rear, Jose being the last man.

279.   M.C.U.  STEPAN.   TRAVEL SHOT

He is running; he looks grim.

280.   MED. SHOT.  VARNOFF.

He is sweating; he wipes his forehead with his sleeve
as he runs.

281.   MED. L.S.   THE PATH NEAR THE BOAR TRAIL CROSSING

The hunters are running along.

282.   MED. SHOT.  THE CROSSING

Diego comes to the place where the wild boar trail
crosses the path; he stops; the others join him.

                    STEPAN
          What is it?

                    DIEGO
                    (Pointing)
          Tracks on path - and boar trail...

Looking down the boar trail Diego spies the piece of
cloth Steve left on the bush.  His face splits in a
triumphant grin.

                    DIEGO
          Look!...There!

He sets off down the trail - towards the bush...

283.  MED. SHOT.  THE TRAIL.  REVERSE ANGLE.  ACROSS THE
      CLOTH ON THE BUSH IN F. G. TO THE HUNTERS IN B.G.

Diego is running towards the peice of cloth; he has
almost reached it - when suddenly he crashes through
the flimsy covering over the trap, and disappears...
The others immediately rush toward the trap - recoil-
ing slightly, when a hideous, piercing shriek resounds
from the depth of the pit.  Hurriedly the men tear the
branch-and-leaf cover aside exposing the entire hole
- while the screams from below are getting ever
weaker.  Finally they stare into the pit - horror
mirrored on their faces.

284.  THE BOTTOM OF THE PIT

Diego is lying on the bottom; around him is coiled
loop upon loop of the huge, enraged python, slowly,
inexorably crushing the life from the man; the blood
is squeezed into his face - bloating it; his eyes
are straining to leave their sockets; in a hoarse,
rasping whisper Diego pleads:

                    DIEGO
          Help...Coronel Stepan...Help me...

285.  MED. CLOSE SHOT.  THE PIT RIM

Stepan carefully raises his rifle; aims - and shoots
into the pit.  Zabala and the sweating Varnoff are
watching.

                    VARNOFF
          Got it!

286.  BOTTOM OF TRAP

The python is dead - its head is blown to pits; it
is still tritching feebly, but Diego is slowly and
painfully shrugging off the great coils; with deep
revulsion he crawls as far away from the twitching,
dead serpent as he can - to huddle against the side
of the trap; he is obviously in great pain; his
chest appears to be crushed, a small trickle of

                                        (CONT.)

blood oozes from the corner of his mouth; one arm
hangs loosely at his side - broken, useless.  Piti-
fully he looks up at the men above.

> DIEGO
> Get me up!...Please get me up...

287.  MED. SHOT.  THE RIM

The four men stand looking down into the trap; no one
moves - they seem transfixed.  Diego's pleadings come
feebly from the pit.

> ZABALA
> (Quietly)
> His chest is crushed...His arm
> broken...

> DIETRICH
> (With annoyance)
> Now we'll have to carry him!

288.  C.U. STEPAN

He looks up sharply at Dietrich's remark; then he looks
back to the path - then down into the pit from where
the pitiful pleas of Diego drift up; his face sets
in grim determination; his hard eyes narrow...

289.  CLOSE GROUP SHOT.  JOSE AND CARGADORES

They all look fearful.

290.  MED. SHOT.  THE RIM

The men are still looking down at Diego, whose pleadings
are taking on a frightened urgency.  Slowly Stepan
raises his rifle; aims - and lets off a single shot...

Diego's pleas stop abruptly...!

291.  MED. SHOT.  JOSE AND THE CARGADORES

They are stunned with shock.  Stepan turns to Jose.

> STEPAN
> Jose!  You track!

292.  M.C.U. JOSE.

He looks petrified; he shakes his head violently.

> JOSE
> No!  No...not know how!

293. GROUP SHOT

The natives are huddled together in fright.

                    STEPAN
                  (Angrily)
          Get the boys moving!

The cargadores huddle closer to the ground; Stepan
turns to Varnoff standing behind them.

                    STEPAN
              Varnoff!

Varnoff grimly raises his rifle, pointing it towards
the cargadores; the natives spring to their feet.
Without another word Stepan whirls on his heels and
heads into the jungle - taking up the pursuit.  The
others follow.

294. EXT. DAY.  NARROW JUNGLE TRAIL.  CLOSE SHOT.  BIG
     IGUANO LIZARD

The nearly six-foot-reptile is laxily dozing in the
sun; faint noises can be heard as someone approaches
through the jungle; suddenly the lizard raises its
head alertly - listens for a brief moment, and quickly
runs off in alarm into the thicket...Camera pulls back
to a MED. L.S.  Down the trail come Coman, Steve and
Nita, followed by Eneepe...They are tired - but still
half-run along the narrow, apparently unused trail...

295. CLOSER ANGLE.  COMAN

He runs easily down the trail...Suddenly he stops -
drops to one knee - and holds up a hand to stop the
others.  They all stop; Steve runs to Coman and kneels
by him.

296. TWO SHOT.  COMAN AND STEVE

                    STEVE
            (In an urgent whisper)
          What is it?

Coman motions him silent; he points ahead; Steve looks.

                    COMAN
              (In a whisper)
          Neipi!

297. MED. L.S.  STEVE'S P.O.V.

Ahead on the trail there is a small sunny spot; a large snake lies there, sunning itself.

298. TWO SHOT.  COMAN AND STEVE

                    STEVE
          A bushmaster...!  We can scare
          it off...

He starts up; Coman grabs him.

                    COMAN
                 (Sharply)
          No!

Steve looks at him.

                    COMAN
          We can use!

                    STEVE
          We can't make another snake trap...

                    COMAN
          Wait...you see...

He looks at Steve with fierce pride; his attitude is still not friendly - and more one of competition with Steve, than cooperation.

                    COMAN (CONT)
          Now Coman make man trap!

299. WIDER ANGLE

Coman motions to Eneepe; the two of them quietly move off the trail a little and Coman whispers instructions to his son, while Nita moves up to Steve.

300. TWO SHOT.  NITA AND STEVE

                    NITA
                 (Also whispering)
          What's wrong?

                    STEVE
          There's a bushmaster wiper on the
          trail...The most venomous snake in
          the jungle...

                    NITA
          What's Coman doing?

                              STEVE
                           (Frowning)
              He wants to make another trap...
              We shouldn't take the time - but
              we do need a rest...

        They both look towards the two Indians.

301.    MED. L.S.  P.O.V.  STEVE AND NITA

        On the trail ahead Coman and Eneepe separate, and slow-
        ly approach the dozing viper...Eneepe from the front -
        Coman from the back.

302.    CLOSER ANGLE

        Eneepe - in front of the snake - makes a small noise;
        the snake at once lifts its head, and stares towards
        him...Slowly - out of reach - Eneepe moves back and
        forth - holding the attention of the deadly reptile...
        and quietly, cautiously Coman steals up behind the
        snake....a heavy rock in his hand...closer and closer...
        Finally he lifts the rock over his head - and crashes
        it down, breaking the reptile's back!  Steve and Nita
        run towards the Indians...

303.    ANOTHER ANGLE

        Steve and Nita come up to Coman and Eneepe; Eneepe
        steps up to Steve; he holds out his hand.

                              ENEEPE
                    Knife!

        Steve hands him the little woman's knife - and Eneepe
        takes off...Coman has laid a big, flat, ugly head of
        the dead bushmaster across a smooth rock...He takes
        a smaller rock in his hand, lifts it up - and crashes
        it down on the snake's head, crushing it! - again -
        and again...

304.    CLOSE TWO SHOT.  STEVE AND NITA

        At the moment of impact Nita turns to Steve in revul-
        sion and horror and buries her face on his shoulder;
        almost at once she realizes what she is doing, and
        draws away...

                              NITA
                    How...can he?...!

                              STEVE
              Coman knows what he's doing...
              Look!

        She looks.

305. MED. SHOT.  P.O.V.  NITA AND STEVE

Eneepe comes up to Coman; he has several small sharply
pointed bamboo splinters, which he has cut...He gives
them to Coman...

306. CLOSE SHOT.  COMAN

One by one Coman dips the bamboo splinters in the
crushed pulp of the snake's head.

307. TWO SHOT.  STEVE AND NITA

                    STEVE
          He crushed the snake's venom sacks...
          Those bamboo splinters will be deadly
          poisonous!...

308. MED. SHOT

Coman and Eneepe are carefully "planting" the poisoned
bamboo splinters in the earth on the trail, hiding
them with grass and weeds...Steve and Nita walk over
to the dead snake.

                    STEVE
          He sure caught on fast...I'm glad
          he's on our side!

He takes hold of the dead snake - and heaves it into
the thicket; Coman and Eneepe have finished their
lethal trap; they come up to Steve; Eneepe gives him
back the knife.

                    STEVE
          (To Coman; with a big grin)
          You're okay, Coman!...Now - let's go!

Coman's face splits in a wide grin - the first time
we've ever seen him smile...He turns to his son - and
unconsciously imitates Steve -

                    COMAN
          Let's go!

They start off down the trail.

Camera slowly pans off them down to a CLOSE SHOT of
the trail...Many little wetly gleaming points can
barely be made out...

309. EXT. DAY.  JUNGLE TREES.  MED. L.S.

A group of monkeys are fleeing through the leafy branches - shrieking, scolding and chattering...

310.  CLOSE SHOT.  GROUND ON TRAIL

The alarmed commotion of the monkeys can be heard -
dying away in the distance...On the trail we can make
out the poisoned bamboo slivers...

Camera pans off the ground to a MED. SHOT down the
trail...Rounding the bend Stepan comes into view;
carrying his rifle at port arms he runs along the
trail; he is followed by Dietrich, Varnoff, Jose and
the three cargadores, and Zabala...  Stepan is
nearing the trapped area...

311.  CLOSE SHOT.  GROUND ON TRAIL

The poisoned splinters are there - waiting...Suddenly
a pair of heavy, black boots come crashing over the
trail...One or two of the venemous spikes are crushed
under the thick soles of the boots!...And another pair
of boots clumps through, destroying yet another few
splinters...

312.  MED. SHOT.  TRAIL

The hunters are trotting down the trail...Suddenly
one of the cargadores leaps into the air with a
hideous shriek and falls to the ground - writhing
in agony!  The men stop at once; Jose and the other
cargadores huddle together in petrified fear; Stepan
runs to the fallen native.

313.  CLOSER SHOT

Stepan bends over the writhing man; he is quickly
joined by Varnoff and Zabala; the native is foaming
at the mouth; he goes into convulsions - and suddenly
relaxes - dead!

Dietrich joins them; he holds out a small object to
Stepan.

                    DIETRICH
                    (Grimly)
            Take a look at this!

Stepan takes the object.

314.  C.U. STEPAN

He is holding the object Dietrich gave him in his
hand and looking at it; it is one of the poisoned
bamboo splinters.

                    STEPAN
            Poisoned!

317.   MED. SHOT

> DIETRICH
> The trail is full of them!

> VANNOFF
> (Incredulously)
> They're setting traps...for us!

> DIETRICH
> Savages!

> STEPAN
> (He gets a hard glint in
> his eyes)
> We are no longer merely hunting
> down a defenseless quarry, gentlemen...
> It's cunning...
> (He holds up the splinter; then
> throws it away)
> against power, now...
> (He pats his rifle)
> and reason!...

> ZABALA
> (He is uneasy)
> We should have gone after them
> right away - like I said...They
> wouldn't have had time for - this...

> STEPAN
> (Sharply)
> You are a fool, Zabala!  If we had
> lost them then - without being
> prepared to hunt them down...We
> might have lost everything!

318.   TWO SHOT.  STEPAN AND ZABALA

Zabala wets his lips nervously.

> ZABALA
> Are you - going on...?

> STEPAN
> (Angrily)
> Of course!

> ZABALA
> They will set other traps!

> STEPAN
> They will!

                    ZABALA
                 (Frightened now)
        But - how will we know...?

                    STEPAN
                  (Coldly)
        We won't!  We'll have to keep
        alert...They must be caught!  We
        can't allow them - or the document -
        to fall into American hands...or
        we will be the ones who are hunted!

319.  GROUP SHOT

                    VARNOFF
        We'll be slowed down...

                    STEPAN
        So will they!  We will not be
        hasty...Patience is a hunter's
        weapon!
          (His tone grows commanding)
        Alright!  Varnoff!  Zabala!  Get the
        men on their feet!  Dietrich!  Take
        point!

        Varnoff and Zabala prod and bully Jose and the frighten
        ed cargadores to their feet; they gingerly skirt the
        trail; Dietrich warily starts down the trail...the
        others follow him.

320.  EXT. DAY.  L.S.  JUNGLE SWAMP

        The riotous swamp vegetation is fantastically luxuriant
        and wild; the four exhausted fugitives are making their
        way through the muddy, slimy morass.

321.  CLOSER ANGLE. SWAMP POOL

        The party reaches a deeper pool in the swamp area; the
        murky water looks forbidding and dark...Coman enters
        the water and starts to wade across the pool.

322.  MED. TWO SHOT.  STEVE AND NITA

        Nita looks with apprehension at the slimy water; Steve
        senses her fear and holds out his hand to her; she
        ignores it; Steve wades a little way out - and turns
        to wait to assist the girl across...Nita cautiously
        starts into the water - when Eneepe comes up to her
        timidly...

                    ENEEPE
                 (Shaking his head)
        No...no!...

323.  CLOSE TWO SHOT.  NITA AND ENEEPE

Nita turns to the boy.

                    NITA
          What is it, Eneepe?

Eneepe makes stroking motion down his arms.

                    ENEEPE
          Linta...Linta!...

He points to Nita's arms and makes a stroking motions
again; when Nita does not understand him, he begins
to pull down her rolled up blouse sleeves...

                    ENEEPE
          Linta!

Nita finally understands what he wants her to do; she
rolls down her sleeves.

                    NITA
          What is - Linta?

                    ENEEPE
          (He points to the water)
          You see...

324.  MED. SHOT

Eneepe quickly enters the swamp water and starts across
to Coman; Nita goes to Steve and follows him across
the chest-high water...

325.  ANOTHER ANGLE.  MED. SHOT.  FAR SIDE OF SWAMP POOL

Steve and Nita are wading ashore; Coman and Eneepe
are already there; they are making curious motions,
as if they were plucking burrs from their skin;
Nita looks questioningly at Steve - and screams!

326.  CLOSE TWO SHOT.  STEVE AND NITA

From Steve's arm dangles a large, fat leech, its
glistening black body slowly writhing!  Nita looks
horror-stricken; Steve turns his arm - and a couple
more leeches can be seen; he grabs at the disgusting
creatures - but Coman steps up to him and stops him.

                    COMAN
          No!  No pull. Squeeze head...so...

He takes a firm grip with two fingers on the leech -
close to the skin.

327.  CLOSE SHOT.  LEECH.

Coman squeezes the leech off Steve's arm.

328.  MED. SHOT

Coman is removing the other leeckes from Steve; Nita -
pale with shock and exhaustion - sits down on a half-
rotted log...

329.  CLOSE SHOT.  NITA

As she sits down her trouser leg slides up a bit - and
with a choked cry the girl crams her fist into her
mouth...Just below the cuff on her leg can be seen the
fat, slimy, writhing body of a leech!

Camera pulls out as Steve rushes to Nita's side; quickly
he raises both trouser legs;  four or five glistening
leeches can be seen; Nita looks away in revulsion;
she is trembling as Steve quickly squeezes off the
repulsive parasites.

330.  C.U.  NITA

Her eyes are closed; her face is strained, as she
attempts to cope with the horror of the leeches.

331.  TWO SHOT

Steve has finished; he rolls down the trouser legs;
he looks up at the trembling girl.

                    STEVE
                  (Quietly)
            Nita...

Slowly the girl turns to him.

                    STEVE
            It's all over...

Nita stands up; she turns away...

332.  ANOTHER ANGLE.  WIDER SHOT

Coman calls:

                    COMAN
            Come!  Must go!

Steve turns to Nita.

                              STEVE
                    We have to go on...

          Nita nods; she follows Steve, as he goes towards Coman
          and Eneepe.

334.   ANOTHER SHOT.  SWAMP POOL BANK

          And there is another swamp pool to be crossed!  Coman
          and Eneepe start across; Steve and Nita come to the
          bank; they stop; Steve steps into the water; Nita
          stays on the bank; her face mirrors all the horror
          and loathing of having to enter the water again...

335.   CLOSE TWO SHOT

          Gravely Steve holds out his hand to Nita; for a moment
          the girl stands stock still - then slowly she takes
          Steve's hand - and enters the water with him - start-
          ing to wade across...

336.   REVERSE ANGLE.  ACROSS COMAN AND ENEEPE ON THE FAR BANK
       TO STEVE AND NITA APPROACHING THROUGH THE SWAMP POOL

          Coman suddenly calls to them.

                              COMAN
                    You come - quick!

          He points off.

337.   MED. L.S. POOL BANK

          On the slimy, muddy bank lie a few crocodiles; as we
          watch one or two of them slither into the water.

338.   TWO SHOT.  STEVE AND NITA

          Steve has seen the reptiles - he quickens the pace
          across the pool.

339.   SHOT

          Crocodile swimming rapidly through the water.

340.   MED. SHOT

          Steve and Nita reach the bank; Coman and Eneepe help
          them up; in the water not far behind them can be seen
          a couple of crocodiles swimming towards them.  Camera
          pans the four fugitives a little away from the bank;
          Nita sinks down to rest...Suddenly there is a flutter-
          ing noise above...They all look up.

341. SHOT. JUNGLE TREES. HIGH BRANCHES

A large bird is settling down on a branch; it is a wild turkey (or other big tropical bird).

342. MED. GROUP SHOT.

Coman - watching the bird steadily - holds out his hand towards Eneepe.

                    COMAN
          Eneepe!

The boy hands him the little toy blowgun and a couple of darts.

343. CLOSE SHOT. COMAN

He inserts the dart in the blowgun; aims - and expels the dart with great force towards the bird...

Camera whip-pans with the dart to a shot of the bird; it gives a mighty flutter - and crashes to the ground.

344. MED. GROUP SHOT

Eneepe runs to pick up the dead burd; he brings it to Coman.

                    STEVE
          Good shot, Coman!

Coman grunts; he takes the bird; steps to the bank of the pool - and hurls the bird far into the water.

345. SHOT. POOL

As the bird hits the surface there is an instant, violent churning of the water, as a couple of crocodiles fight over the prey...

346. MED. SHOT. GROUP

                    STEVE
                  (Shocked)
          Hey! What are you doing? We
          could use that!

                    COMAN
                  (Imperturbedly)
          Better use! Keep crocodiles here
          long time...
                  (He nods back)
          For them!

Coman looks up at the sky.

                    COMAN
            Come.  We leave swamp.  Jungle
            soon dark.

    They start off.

                                        DISSOLVE

347.    EXT. DUSK.  JUNGLE SWAMP. L.S.

    The hunters - led by Stepan and Dietrich have reached
    the crocodile pool; in the sluggish water several of
    the ugly reptiles can be seen swimming about - still
    agitated by the bait thrown them by Coman; Stepan and
    Dietrich pause at the bank.

348.    CLOSE SHOT

    Crocodile swimming in the murky water.

349.    MED. TWO SHOT.  STEPAN AND DIETRICH

    Stepan raises his rifle.

                    STEPAN
            Let's clear them out!...

    He fires at a crocodile; Dietrich follows suit.

350.    SHOT

    Crocodile - hit by a bullet - chruning up the water as
    it thrashes about.

351.    TWO SHOT.  STEPAN AND DIETRICH

    They are firing; behind them the others are waiting -
    Jose and the cargadores in fearful agitation, kept
    under control by Varnoff and Zabala.

352.    EXT. DUSK.  JUNGLE.  C.U. COMAN

    He looks intent; he is listening; his nostrils are
    dilated as he strains every sense; in the far distance
    a couple of shots ring out.

353.    TWO SHOT.  STEVE AND NITA

    They look at each other gravely.

                    STEVE
            The crocodiles...They've reached
            the swamp!

354.  MED. SHOT.  (COMAN, STEVE, NITA AND ENEEPE)

Coman turns and resumes making his way through the jungle; the others follow.

355.  EXT. DUSK.  SWAMP POOL.  MED. SHOT

Stepan and Dietrich start across the crocodile infested water; Varnoff and Zabala herd Jose and the two remaining cargadores into the water - and start out themselves flanking them.

356.  CLOSE SHOT

Stepan is making his way through the slimy, chest-high swamp water.

357.  ANGLE FROM FAR BANK TO APPROACHING MEN

Stepan and Dietrich are almost across; the others are following them; in the B.G. one of the cargadores - carrying his burden on his head like the others - has fallen a little behind...

Suddenly he lets out a gruesome, anguished scream, drops his burden and flails his arms in the air, and almost at once he disappears below the surface of the churning water!  The other cargadores immediately drop their burdens and make for the bank as fast as they can in utter panic;  Varnoff and Zabala turn and fire a couple of shots - to no avail...

358.  CLOSE SHOT. CHURNING WATER

As we watch the murky, swirling water the arm of the hapless cargador breaks the surface and reaches up into the air - and hand making desperate attempts to grasp the empty space...Then it slowly is drawn below the surface - to disappear...

359.  MED. SHOT.  BANK

The rest of the hunters have reached the safety of the bank; they are staring grimly at the slowly quieting water, where the native was pulled under; Jose and the last cargador are petrified with shock, huddled together...Stepan looks up at the darkening sky.

                    STEPAN
          It will be dark in a minute...We'll
          camp here...

                    VARNOFF
          We'd better catch up with them
          tomorrow...

                         STEPAN
                        (Coldly)
                We'd better!  Thanks to your
                stupidity Steve Carter is very
                well informed!

                                        DISSOLVE

360.  EXT. NIGHT.  JUNGLE.  BASE OF LARGE TREE.  CLOSE SHOT.
      MARKED MAP OF CANAL ZONE.

      It is night; the jungle is dark - except for a few
      patches of moonlight seeping down through the thick,
      leafy roof of branches.  Spread out on the ground in
      one such patch is a map of the Canal Zone with
      numerous markings on it.  From a CLOSE SHOT of this
      map Camera pulls back to a MED. SHOT.  The four
      fugitives are sitting between the large roots of a
      big tree; Steve is examining the map and other docu-
      ments from the case spread out in front of him; Nita
      is watching him gravely; Coman and Eneepe are scraping
      and breaking a few touch looking vegetable roots with
      Steve's little knife.

                         STEVE
                ...It's all here...The whole
                insiduous plot...From A to Z...

361.  TWO SHOT.  STEVE AND NITA

                         STEVE (CONT)
                Stepan and his henchmen...nothing
                but a bunch of greedy mercenaries -
                on a fantastic scale...without
                any scruples or decency...Guns -
                murderers - for hire!...

      Nita turns away; Steve suddenly realizes that the
      objects of his bitter harangue include the girl's late
      father...He stops, begins to stuff the papers back
      into the map case.

                         STEVE
                        (Quietly)
                I'm sorry, Nita...I didn't mean to
                hurt you...

                         NITA
                        (Softly)
                You only did...Because you are right!

362.  WIDER ANGLE

      Eneepe comes over to Nita; he hands her a couple of
      roots.

                        ENEEPE
                Eat...Good for hunger...

Nita turns to him; she has tears in her eyes; she
takes the roots with a little smile of gratitude.

                        NITA
                Thank you, Eneepe.

Eneepe's face breaks into a broad smile; he gives Steve
a root, too, and settles down to watch Nita eat -
himself knawing away contentedly...Camera dollies
in to a THREE SHOT - STEVE, NITA AND ENEEPE...Nita
begins to knaw at the root; she is hungry - but the
root is bitter and tough; she looks unhappy - but
tries to eat...Eneepe's smile turns to a little frown
of concern.

                        STEVE
                    (To Nita)
                Hungry?

The girl nods.

                        STEVE
                Guess we all are...Maybe tomorrow
                we can stop long enough to hunt
                up some food...

                        NITA
                It's alright...I know it is more
                important to go on.

She puts the root aside; she shivers lightly in the
cool, damp jungle night.

363.    WIDER ANGLE

Steve gets up.

                        STEVE
                Try to get some rest...Try to
                sleep...

He sits down close to the girl.

                        STEVE
                Stay close to me...we can't take
                the chance of making a fire...

At first Nita draws away from Steve - but then, slowly,
she huddles up against him...

364.   TWO SHOT.  STEVE AND NITA

Steve tries to make the girl as comfortable as he can;
for a moment their eyes meet; then Nita nowers hers...
But there is a tiny smile of contentment on her lips...

> STEVE
> Tomorrow, Nita...When it's light...
> We'll make a fire...find something
> to eat...

365.   TWO SHOT.  ENEEPE AND COMAN

Eneepe is watching Steve and Nita; he turns to his
father.

> ENEEPE
> (Eagerly)
> Father.  I can get food for us.
> I have seen the burrows of the
> painted rabbit...
> (He points)
> There...

> COMAN
> No, my son.  Stay here.  Do not
> leave the camp.  There is much
> danger.

Eneepe looks at his father seriously, and with disap-
pointment.

> ENEEPE
> But, father...

> COMAN
> Eneepe.  Do not forget the laws
> of the Cuna.  A good son obeys his
> father!

> ENEEPE
> Yes, father...

He looks towards Steve and Nita.

366.   CLOSE SHOT.  ENEEPE

He is watching Steve and Nita; he settles down against
the tree; he looks concerned; his hand finds the little
blowgun and the bunch of darts; he picks them up...For
a moment he looks at them - then a look of resolved
decision settles on his face, as he sinks back to rest.

> DISSOLVE

367.  EXT. SUNRISE SHOT.  X.L.S.  JUNGLE VALLEY

It is a big, scenic shot of a narrow jungle valley;
the sun is just rising on the horizon.

368.  EXT. DAWN.  VALLEY SLOPE, LEFT.  CLOSE SHOT, JUNGLE
THICKET

There is a small movement near a bush; it is Stepan;
he is crouching on the ground; he is looking through
a pair of binoculars - scanning the opposite slope
of the little valley.

369.  CLOSE SHOT.  STEPAN

He is moving the binoculars slowly as he scans the other
slope; suddenly he stops.

370.  SHOT.  SPECIAL EFFECT - AS SEEN THROUGH BINOCULARS.
PAN SHOT.

Held in the circle of the binoculars a small animal
can be seen moving at the edge of a little clearing in
the jungle on the opposite (right) valley slope; it
is a conejo pintado - a 'painted rabbit'; it is
peacefully nibbling at some leafy plants...The
binocular circle slowly moves across the little clearing to the other edge of the clearing; a figure can be
seen stealthily moving there;  it is Eneepe...

371.  CLOSE SHOT.  STEPAN

Behind him can be seen Varnoff, Dietrich and Zabala
Stepan turns around; he signals to the men to show
caution, and motions them to take up positions on
either side of him, indicating to them that their
quarry is just across the little valley...As the
armed men move to obey his instructions, Stepan
takes up his own rifle, checks the telescopic sight
- and aims through it at the opposite valley slope...

372.  SHOT.  SPECIAL EFFECT - AS SEEN THROUGH TELESCOPIC
SIGHT

Through the telescopic sight on Stepan's rifle we see
Eneepe; he is cautiously stealing towards the unsus-
pecting rabbit; the crosshairs of the sight center
directly on the boy; Eneepe stops - completely unaware
of his own danger - and raises the little blowgun to
his mouth...

At that instant a shot rings out; the sight crosshairs
jar slightly - and Eneepe pitches forward to the
ground - motionless.

373. EXT. DAY. CAMP AT BASE OF TREE. CLOSE SHOT. COMAN

The Indian sits up quickly to a C.U.

374. MED. SHOT

Steve, Coman and Nita are alerted; they at once look
around for Eneepe...In the distance two more shots
ring out...then silence...

375. CLOSE SHOT. COMAN

He looks for the blowgun; he sees it is gone..

376. MED. SHOT

Quickly Coman is on his feet; he at once finds the
trail where Eneepe entered the jungle; without a work
he starts after his son - followed by Steve and Nita.

377. EXT. DAY. MED. SHOT. EDGE OF SMALL CLEARING IN JUNGLE
ON VALLEY SLOPE, RIGHT

Coman comes running to the edge of the clearing; he
stops short; Steve and Nita come up to him.

378. THREE SHOT

Nita points out into the clearing.

                    NITA
            There!  Out there!...

379. L.S.  CLEARING.  P.O.V. NITA

In the middle of the small clearing lies Eneepe; he
is still and motionless.

380. GROUP SHOT

Coman moves to run out into the clearing; Steve holds
him back; he points to the other (left) valley slope.

                    STEVE
            Hold it!...They're just waiting
            for us to do that...

381. TWO SHOT  COMAN AND STEVE - OVERLAPPING

                    STEVE
            ...Over there...

                    COMAN
            (He looks seriously at Steve)
            Eneepe is my son.

                                    (CONT.)

381.   CONTINUED

                          STEVE
               Stay here - till they're busy
               with me...Then - go get him!

382,   MED. SHOT

       Steve jumps up and runs out into the clearing; at once
       a couple of shots ring out from the left slope...

383.   L.S.   CLEARING

       Steve is running - broken field - towards the fallen
       Eneepe; several bullets whizz through the air to slam
       into the earth, sometimes mere inches away from the
       darting Steve; Suddenly Steve veers away from Eneepe
       - as if scared off by the shooting, and begins to zig-
       zag for the protecting jungle; the firing follows him...
       At this moment Coman comes racing out from the brush
       cover; he runs straight for Eneepe; reaches him;
       lifts him up - and runs back to the jungle - before the
       riflemen on the far slope can switch target from Steve
       to Coman...

384.   MED. SHOT.   JUNGLE

       Steve - out of breath - comes running through the
       jungle; Camera pans him to the narrow trail, where
       he joins Coman and Nita; Coman is kneeling at the side
       of Eneepe, who is lying on the ground; Nita stands
       by; Steve comes up to her.

385.   TWO SHOT.   STEVE AND NITA.

       Steve looks questioningly at Nita; the girl shakes
       her head gravely.

                          NITA
               He was trying to get food...for
               us...

386.   CLOSE SHOT.   COMAN

       He looks stony-faced; slowly he reaches down and re-
       moves the little blowgun, still clutched firmly in
       Eneepe's hand; he puts it in his belt, as Steve kneels
       beside him - camera widens to a TWO SHOT.

                          STEVE
               Coman

                          COMAN
               My son...
                    (He looks up at Steve)
               Your friend....

386.    CONTINUED

                              STEVE
                    Coman...You must come with us
                    ...Let us put Eneepe to rest...
                        (He indicates a tall tree
                         with a nod of his head)
                    ...up there.

                              COMAN
                    No.

                              STEVE
                    There isn't much time...

                              COMAN
                    You risk your life - when you think
                    to help Eneepe...*Now* he help you.

          He turns to look back across the valley towards the
          hunters...

387.    C.U.  COMAN - OVERLAPPING

          His eyes are blazing.

                              COMAN
                    My son has not yet stopped fighting
                    his enemy!

388.    EXT. DAY.  LEFT VALLEY SLOPE.  MED. WIDE SHOT

          Stepan and his men are starting to cross the valley;
          they are hurrying; Varnoff and Zabala 'ride herd' on
          the cargadores.

                              STEPAN
                        (He is angry)
                    ...You didn't bring down either
                    of them!  What were you shooting
                    at!?

                              DIETRICH
                    You were shooting too, Stepan.

          Stepan fixes him with a dangerous glare; Dietrich
          looks uneasy.

                              DIETRICH
                    It isn't easy to hit a moving
                    target with a telescopic sight...
                    You know that...

388.  CONTINUED

                    STEPAN
          Alright!  Let's get after them.'
          It'll take an hour to cross that
          draw...

They begin to trot off down the slope...

389.  EXT. DAY.  JUNGLE TRAIL.  MED. SHOT

Coman is hurriedly putting the finishing touches to a
crudely made, long bow with a coarse grass-rope bow
string; Steve and Nita are watching him; Coman holds
the bow out to look at it; then he turns to a clump
of heavy bamboo stalks at the side of the trail; Camera
pans with the action; through the bamboo can be seen
dimly the form of a human figure; it is Eneepe; all
that can be made out clearly is one brown bare arm
sticking out from the thick bamboo stand; Coman
carefully places the crude bow in the hand of Eneepe;
then he places a thin bamboo shaft across it, as if
an arrow on the bow was being aimed down the trail.

                    COMAN
          It has no  strength to shoot - this
          bow...My son can not see his enemy...
          We know...But they do not.

He stands up.

                    COMAN
          Come.

He starts down the trail; Steve and Nita follow him;
Camera pans off them to a CLOSE SHOT of the bamboo
stand; the boy can just barely be made out by anyone
coming up the trail; a man in hiding - waiting to let
fly a deadly arrow!

                                        DISSOLVE

390.  EXT. DAY.  JUNGLE CLEARING. CLOSE SHOT.  GROUND

It is the spot where Eneepe died; there is a large,
dark stain on the grass and weed cover; ringing it
stand several pairs of legs in big, black boots...
Camera pull out to a MED. SHOT revealing Stepan and
his three men; they are looking down at the stain;
the cargadores are huddled in the B.G.  Stepan bends
down, dips his fingers in the stain and 'feels' it.

                    ZABALA
          You got him alright...

                                        (CONT.)

390.  CONTINUED

Stepan looks towards the jungle, where Coman disappeared with his son.

                    STEPAN
          Coma on!

The four hunters start running towards the jungle edge; the cargadores remain behind.

391.  EXT. DAY.  JUNGLE TRAIL.  MED. SHOT

Down the trail come the four hunters; Stepan in the lead; he is tracking efficiently and cautiously; he comes to a blind bend in the narrow trail; he stops - and cautiously looks around the bend, down the trail; he starts around the bend, when he suddenly jumps back, and motions for the others to stay back.

392.  FOUR SHOT

The four hunters are crouched together on the trail.

                    VARNOFF
          What is it?

                    STEPAN
          Quiet!  Look for yourself...
          careful!

393.  CLOSE SHOT.  VARNOFF

Cautiously he peers around the bend.

394.  L.S. DOWN TRAIL.  VARNOFF'S P.O.V.

In the distance is the stand of bamboo next to the trail; vaguely the motionless figure of Eneepe can be seen...waiting...arrow on bow!

395.  FOUR SHOT

Varnoff turns to the others.

                    VARNOFF
          Someone's there...Hiding...
          waiting...With a bow and
          arrow...

Stepan nods.

                    DIETRICH
          The boy!

396.  C.U.  DIETRICH - OVERLAPPING

                    DIETRICH

          You only wounded him.  He's been
          left behind - to kill one of us!

397.  FOUR SHOT

                        ZABALA
                      (Nervously)
          Can't we just - go around him?

                        STEPAN
                      (Grimly)
          We can't leave him here - alive...
          Varnoff.  Dietrich.  Circle around
          to the left.  Zabala, stay here.  Take
          your time.  Don't make a sound.  Get
          in position for a clean shot before
          you fire.  I'll take the right flank.
          Get going!

      Slowly, carefully the men start out.,...

                            DISSOLVE

398.  EXT. DAY. SMALL JUNGLE STREAM.  CLOSE SHOT

      The water is swirling and tumbling across some rocks;
      Camera pans to a MED. SHOT.  Steve, Nita and Coman
      are refreshing themselves at the clear water.

399.  THREE SHOT

      Nita is sponging her neck and shoulders with her
      handkerchief; Coman is crouched at the stream drink-
      ing animal style...Suddenly - in the far distance -
      there is a shot...

400.  CLOSE SHOT.  COMAN

      He jerks his head up - and looks grimly back towards
      the sound...There are several more shots in quick
      succession; Coman winces almost imperceptibly.

401.  TWO SHOT.  STEVE AND NITA

      They look at each other soberly.

402.  MED. SHOT.

      Coman stands up - proudly erect.

                              (CONT.)

402.  CONTINUED

                    COMAN
          We go.  My son has given us time.

He turns abruptly, and starts wading down the narrow,
shallow stream.

403.  EXT. DAY.  BAMBOO STAND AT TRAIL.  CLOSE SHOT

Out from the bamboo stand across the trail stretches
the limp arm of Eneepe - holding the make-shift  bow
in his hand; Camera pulls out to a MED. SHOT. Varnoff,
Dietrich and Stepan converge upon the spot; Stepan
picks up the dummy bow - and hurls it away in disgust;
Dietrich looks in the bamboo stand at Eneepe's body;
he turns to Stepan and Varnoff.

                    DIETRICH
                 (Tight-lipped)
          We were tricked!  The boy was dead
          all the time!

404.  CLOSE SHOT.  STEPAN

He looks down at the limp arm.

                    STEPAN
                  (Grimly)
          Three to go...!

405.  MED. SHOT.

Zabala comes running up to the others; he is excited.

                    ZABALA
          Stepan!  The cargadores!  They've
          run away...

                    STEPAN
          What?!

                    ZABALA
          When you started shooting...they
          took off!

                    STEPAN
                  (Sharply)
          Why didn't you stop them?

                    ZABALA
                (Wetting his lips)
          I - I couldn't...

405.    CONTINUED

                    STEPAN
          We don't need them.  Let's go!

He starts down the trail, followed by the three men.

406.    EXT. DAY.  NARROW JUNGLE STREAM.  MED. SHOT.  THE
        FUGITIVES

The going is rough for Nita; Steve is helping her as
best he can; Coman is a little ahead of them. Steve
stops.

                    STEVE
          Coman!

Coman runs back to Steve and Nita, while Steve helps
the exhausted girl to the edge of the narrow stream,
where she sinks down.

407.    TWO SHOT.  STEVE AND COMAN

                    STEVE
          Coman.  We can't outrun Stepan...

Coman grunts.

                    STEVE
          We'll have to fight back...We may
          have a chance if we can keep fighting
          back - not with guns...but with traps!

Coman's attitude towards Steve has undergon a subtle
change; no longer is he hostile and distrustful.

                    COMAN
          I help make trap.

                    STEVE
          Good.  Your son gave us time...time
          to use our one ally - the jungle!
          Let's do it...

408.    MED. SHOT

Steve wades towards a branch, which reaches out over
the little stream about four feet above the surface;
it looks strong and 'springy!.

                    STEVE
          Here.  Let's get busy...

He begins to strip the twigs and leaves off the branch;
he throws his little knife to Coman.

                              (CONT.)

408.	CONTINUED

STEVE
Cut three bamboo spears.  As long
as your arm.  Sharpen them - with
points...

Coman catches the knife; he starts for a bamboo stand.

409.	CLOSE SHOT.  STEVE

He is stripping twigs off the branch, working fast...

DISSOLVE

410.	CLOSE SHOT.  COMAN

He is sharpening the last of three two-foot long
bamboo spears; they look wickedly sharp and pointed.
Coman has a little trouble with his left hand; the
wounds on his wrist are becoming infected; he briefly
bathes the wrist in the cool water...

DISSOLVE

411.	CLOSE SHOT.  STEVE

He is placing a long stick on the water just below the
surface, wedging one end in the rocks, while the other
end reaches up on the stream bank...

DISSOLVE

412.	CLOSE SHOT.  COMAN

He is making a grass rope; he is working fast...

DISSOLVE

413.	CLOSE SHOT.  STEVE

With the knife he is cutting off a low branch on a
squat bush at the edge of the stream; he is whittl-
ing the two-inch long stump left on the trunk smooth
and tapered; he measures the stick reaching from the
stream to reach this stump...

DISSOLVE

414.	MED. SHOT.  TWO SHOT.  COMAN AND STEVE

Steve is testing the grass rope; he puts as much
strain on it as he can; it breaks

(CONT.)

STEVE
It won't hold, Coman...Not strong
enough.

COMAN
Take long time to make strong
grass rope.

Nita comes up to them; she is carrying the document case

NITA
Steve...Will this do?  The strap,
I mean?

Steve takes the case; it has a strong, webbed carrying
strap about four feet long with an iron ring at each
end.

STEVE
That's it!

He takes the case.

STEVE
Just what we need...

415.  CLOSE SHOT.  STEVE

He cuts off the strap from the case so that the iron
rings remain on the strap.

DISSOLVE

416.  CLOSE SHOT.  END OF BRANCH.

The branch has been stripped of twigs and leaves, and
forcefully bend tack to the stream bank; the three
bamboo spears cut by Coman have been tied, cross-fash-
ion, on the branch end with grass rope about ten inches
apart; like needle-sharp stilettos they point outward,
so that when the branch is allowed to swing out over the
 stream it carries with it three murderous daggers -
just about a man's heart height!  At the very tip
of the branch one of the iron rings of the strap has
been fastened, holding the taut, bent branch in place;
the strap itself carries across another branch and then
down towards the ground...

Camera pulls back to a MED. SHOT to reveal Steve and
Nita; Steve is inspecting the cross-tied spears...
He turns towards the stream.

STEVE
Is the trip stick in place?

417. ANOTHER ANGLE

In the stream in the F.G. is Coman; in the B.G. on the
right bank of the stream Steve and Nita can be seen,
next to the bent back and concealed branch; Coman
bends down.

418.

CLOSE PAN SHOT. TRIP STICK

The stick Steve placed in the stream can be seen reaching up to the bank; Camera pans along it to see that it
rests on the smooth stump cut on the bush by Steve;
it rests between the trunk - and the other end of the
webbed strap, the iron ring of which is precariously
gripping the very tip of the tapering stump; the slight-
est jar on the trip stick, and the ring will slip off
- releasing the powerful, bend branch, sending it
whipping out across the stream with its deadly stilettos!

419. WIDER ANGLE

Coman is crouched in the F.G.  Steve and Nita are on
the bank in the B.G.

                    COMAN
          Stick is ready!

                    STEVE
          Alright, Coman...Trip it!

Cautiously Coman reaches out and touches the stick...
Immediately there is a whooshing sound; the branch
comes whipping out from its camouflaged positions with
tremendous force a couple of feet over the crouching
Coman's head; the three needle-sharp daggers gleam
murderously...

420. CLOSE SHOT.  BRANCH END WITH BAMBOO SPEARS

The branch whips back and forth with its leathal burden,
slowing down to hang quivering over the stream.

WIDER ANGLE

Steve, Nita and Coman come splashing up to the branch.

                    STEVE
          It works.  Let's set it again - and
          get out of here!

He begins to bend the powerful branch spring back
towards the stream bank.

                    DISSOLVE

421. EXT. DAY.  SMALL JUNGLE STREAM.  CLOSE SHOT

It is the same shot as before; the water is swirling
and tumbling across the rocks; Camera again pans to
a MED. SHOT down the stream.  Stepan, Dietrich,
Varnoff and Zabala are looking around the stream and
banks to try to find their quarry's tracks.  Varnoff
is furthest down stream; suddenly he calls.

                    VARNOFF
          Stepan!  Here!...

The men run towards him.

422. CLOSER ANGLE

Stepan and the others reach Varnoff; he points to some
water weeds growing near the bank.

                    VARNOFF
          There...look...

423. CLOSE SHOT.  WEEDS

Several of the stalks are broken - all pointing downstream.

424. MED. SHOT

                    STEPAN
          They're going downstream...

Varnoff turns to splash down the stream; the others
follow.

425. EXT. DAY.  STREAM.  TRAP AREA.  SHOOTING ANGLE:
UP STREAM

In the B.G. the hunters approach, led by Varnoff, who
is constantly looking at the stream bottom as he
splashes on - closer and closer to the trap...

426. ANOTHER ANGLE.  CLOSER SHOT

Varnoff is almost at the trap.

427. CLOSE SHOT.  VARNOFF'S FEET

The big, black boots are splashing through the shallow
water; the trip stick is just before them - and a
heavy boot kicks it loose...!

428. MED. SHOT. VARNOFF

At once there is the familiar whoosh - and the trap
branch whips out and carches Varnoff full in the chest!
Varnoff screams hoarsely - once...

429. QUICK C.U. STEPAN

His eyes are wide; he looks stunned.

430. QUICK C.U. ZABALA

He looks sick with horror and fear.

431. MED. SHOT

The three men run to Varnoff; he is hanging limply
on the sturdy branch, sagging into the water so that
it looks as if he is kneeling; one of the bamboo
spears has penetrated his chest completely - another
his arm; he is dead...

432. M.C.U. STEPAN

He looks at the dead man; his expression is dark - and
a flicker of fear can be seen in his eyes.

433. MED. SHOT

The three horrified men are standing around Varnoff;
Dietrich tentatively tries to free the man from the
bamboo spears.

                    STEPAN
                   (Grimly)
        Leave him.  We have no time to waste.

Abruptly he turns and wades down the stream; Dietrich
follows - and, reluctantly, Zabala...leaving Varnoff
hanging on the deadly branch...

Camera pans down to a CLOSE SHOT of Varnoff's legs;
his knees are almost resting on the stream bottom,
the big, black boots stretching out in the water
ineffectually...A dark stain is spreading in the
clear stream - and is being  washed away downstream...

                              DISSOLVE.

434. EXT. NIGHT.  SHOT OF NIGHT SKY.  PAN SHOT

The clear, starry night sky can be seen through a
hole in the jungle tree cover.  Camera pans down to
a MED SHOT of a little hollow; Steve is lying on the

                              (CONT.)

343.    CONTINUED

incline, watching intently through the underbrush;
the jungle is filled with the night noises; Steve
slides down into the hollow to join Nita; Camera
moves in to a CLOSE TWO SHOT.

                    NITA
Not uet?

                    STEVE
He'll be back...

                    NITA
          (Anxiously)
You don't think - he's left us?

                    STEVE
          (Thoughtfully)
No.  No - I trust Coman.

                    NITA
Do you think...Are they still
following us?

                    STEVE
You can be sure of that!

                    NITA
          (With a little sigh)
Wouldn't it be wonderful - if they'd
turned back...?

                    STEVE
Yes - wonderful...But wonderful things
don't happen just because they're wonderful...They happen because they're
possible...And Stepan couldn't possibly
let us go!....

                    NITA
But - the traps...They will keep him
from catching us...Will they not?

                    STEVE
They'll make him cautious...Slow him
down...But they also take time to make...

Nita looks at him with large, frightened eyes; he
smiles at her, encouragingly.

                    STEVE
We'll make it...But we're stretching
our luck pretty far...

                              (CONT.)

434.   CONTINUED

                    NITA
          Stretching - our luck?

                    STEVE
          I only hope we won't stretch it so
          far it snaps right bank and knocks
          our teeth in!

                    NITA
          I - don't understand...

                    STEVE
               (With a little smile)
          Just as well...

                    NITA
          You know how to make Indian traps...
          You  can speak with Coman in his tongue
          ...Yet - you are American?

                    STEVE
          It's my business to know about primitive
          people, Nita...
                    (Musingly)
          Someone once asked what earthly good
          that could be...I guess I've found one
          answer anyway...

                    NITA
          Was she pretty?

                    STEVE
               (Startled)
          Who?

                    NITA
          The girl - who didn't like your -
          business?

                    STEVE
          Yes.  She was pretty...

Nita looks down; Steve suddenly seems  to become aware
of Nita as a beautiful girl for the first time; he
looks at her curiously...

                    STEVE (CONT.)
          ...In a way...I wonder how she'd have
          made out...here...

Nita looks up at Steve; they are regarding each other
gravely - when suddenly there is a small noise.

435. WIDER ANGLE

Steve and Nita start, as Coman comes sliding down into
the hollow; he carries a dead Iguano lizard and a small
bunch of unripe bananas, he throws them in front of
Steve and Nita.

                      COMAN
                   (Beaming)
      Food!

Nita looks with revulsion at the lizard; Camera zooms
in to a CLOSE SHOT of the dead reptile.

436. THREE SHOT

Coman reaches for Steve's knife; he picks up the lizard;
prepares to cut it.

437. CLOSE TWO SHOT

Nita looks almost sick with repugnance; she turns away,
looks at Steve.

                      NITA
      I - can't...

                     STEVE
      Try, Nita...You need strength.

                      NITA
      Raw?

                     STEVE
      We can't risk a fire...

Nita looks miserable; she glances towards Coman; quickly
she turns back to Steve and buries her head on his
shoulder; Steve puts his arm around the girl's shoulders; he looks down at her tenderly, and kisses her
hair lightly.

                     STEVE
                  (Softly)
      Easy, Nita...We'll make it...

Camera dollies in to a C.U. of STEVE; he looks worried.

                     DISSOLVE

438. INT. NIGHT. DUNCAN'S OFFICE. C.U. CUNDAN. PULL
BACK TO A MED. SHOT.

Duncan is standing in front of the wall map of Panama.

                     (CONT)

438.   CONTINUED

                         DUNCAN
              I admit - I am a little worried...

Camera pulls out to reveal Harrison, Mendez and Col.
Bankes seated around Duncan's desk; Duncan goes to
his desk.

                         HARRISON
              It's been five days since the
              last radio contact?

                         DUNCAN
              Yes.

                         HARRISON
              Any indications of trouble then?

                         DUNCAN
              None

                         BANKES
              I don't think there's any cause
              for immediate concern...Probably
              only equipment breakdown...

                         HARRISON
              Perhaps...Mr. Mendez.  Through your
              office will you instruct your National
              Police Force to be on the look-out for
              our men...should they make contact at
              some small village?

                         MENDEZ
              Of course.

                         BANKES
              All Emergency Landing Fields along
              both the Panama coast lines have
              already been alerted...

                         DUNCAN
              Col. Bankes and I are leaving for
              Albrook Field tomorrow...

                         HARRISON
              Have you given any thought to your
              course of action, if no contact is
              established in the near future?

Duncan walks back to the wall mpa; he looks worried.

439.  M.C.U.  DUNCAN

                    DUNCAN
          There's very little we <u>can</u> do...
          if something <u>has</u> happened to them...
               (He turns to the map)
          They could be <u>anywhere</u> in there...

Camera dollies in across Duncan to a CLOSE SHOT of the
jungle section on the map.

                    DUNCAN (CONT)
          Our chances of finding them would
          be almost nil...

                              DISSOLVE

440.  EXT. DAY.  L.S.  JUNGLE

It is a scenic shot from a high spot out over the sea
of green, which is the virgin jungle of Panama.

441.  EXT. DAY.  JUNGLE CLEARING.  M.L.S.

A steep, rocky cliff borders one side of the clearing;
the jungle the others; a little spring trickles down the
cliff side; Steve, Nita and Coman are gathered around
it.

442.  THREE SHOT

All three fugitives look tired and worn; Steve is
examining Coman's injured wrist; the wound has closed,
but it is so badly infected that it is swollen so much
that Coman hardly can move his hand; Nita is ripping
off one of her shirt sleeves, tearing it into strips
and moistening it in the cool spring water.

                    STEVE
               (Concerned)
          It's very badly infected...It'll
          have to be taken care of - soon...

Nita brings the cloth.

                    NITA
          This may help take down the swelling.

She begins to bandage the wounded wrist.

                    STEVE
          Coman.  How long before we hit
          the coast?

                    COMAN
          One day - two...

442. CONTINUED

                         STEVE
          Two days...We can't keep running
          all the time...But if we don't -
          they'll catch up with us...

                         NITA
          Couldn't we set another trap?

                         STEVE
          By now Stepan's probably too cautious
          to fall for anything we can rig up...

Nita has finished the bandage.

                         NITA
          Suppose - suppose we baited the
          trap?

                         STEVE
          With what?

Nita picks up the document case.

                         NITA
          This.

Steve's eyes light up.

                         STEVE
          Hey!  It might work!  If Stepan
          thought we'd dropped the documents
          - he'd stop to pick them up...

                         NITA
          And you would have made a trap!

                         STEVE
          It'll have to be one whopper of a
          booby trap to hook him at this stage
          of the game!...
               (He looks around)
          Coman.  How much time have we got?

                         COMAN
          They perhaps two - three hours behind.

                         STEVE
               (Resolutely)
          It's worth a gamble...I remember a
          pretty tricky booby trap I saw in
          Korea...You'll both have to give me
          a hand...I think maybe we can outwit
          Colonel Stepan!

442.   CONTINUED

He begins urgently to explain to Nita and Coman what
he has in mind...

DISSOLVE

443.   EXT. DAY.   JUNGLE CLEARING.   SHOT

Stepan comes trotting across the clearing, passing
Camera in a M.C.U., closely followed by Zabala and
Dietrich; all three men look drawn and tense; Stepan
almost frantic...

444.   MED. SHOT

The three men are half-running across the clearing;
they look around warily; it is the clearing that is
bordered on one side by the steep, rocky cliff, and
by the jungle on the others; a few trees and clumps
of shrubbery dot the clearing...Suddenly Dietrich
stops.

DIETRICH
Stepan!  Over there!...

He points towards the cliff; Stepan and Zabala stop
and look.

445.   SHOT.  P.O.V.  DIETRICH

In the grass directly in front of him, not thirty feet
away, near the rock wall, lies the document case;
in its half-open mouth can be seen a white paper...

446.   THREE SHOT

DIETRICH
They dropped the documents!

He moves to run towards the case;  Stepan stops him.

STEPAN
Wait!  It may be another trap.

Dietrich stops shot; he scowls.

ZABALA
Let's just leave them there...
There's no reason to take a chance
- if it is a trap...!

STEPAN
We can't leave them.  There are
villages within a day or two of
here.  They might be found.

(CONT)

446. CONTINUED

                    DIETRICH
          There's nothing around it...I'm
          sure it's safe...

                    STEPAN
          Look again, Dietrich...The branches
          of that tree...They extend out over
          the case...

447. L.S. DOCUMENT CASE. P.O.V. STEPAN - OVERLAPPING

                    STEPAN (O.S.)
          Anything could be rigged to fall
          from there - including poison darts
          ...And that thick brush...

448. THREE SHOT - OVERLAPPING

                    STEPAN
          ...A drawn bow could be hidden there...

                    ZABALA
          I say let's forget about the papers!

Stepan lifts up his binoculars.

                    STEPAN
          Let's take a closer look...

He looks through the binoculars.

449. SHOT. DOCUMENT CASE. SPECIAL EFFECT. AS SEEN THROUGH
BINOCULARS.

The case looms large in the circle of the eyepieces;
the binoculars move to the overhanging branches; nothing
can be seen; it moves to the brush; again nothing; it
searches out the ground around the case - and suddenly
stops. There - clearly seen through the binoculars -
is a taut grass rope running from the case towards the
tree trunk!

                    STEPAN (O.S.)
          Ah!  I thought so.'

450. THREE SHOT

Stepan lowers the binoculars.

                    STEPAN
          There's a grass rope - a trip rope
          - running from the case to that tree.
          It is trapped!

                              (CONT.)

450.   CONTINUED

> DIETRICH
> I don't see how...With what?
>
> STEPAN
> Have you forgotten where the
> prisoners were before they
> escaped?
>
> DIETRICH
> The cave?
>
> STEPAN
> Exactly.
>
> DIETRICH
> (With realization)
> The handgrenades!  They could've
> found the grenades!
>
> ZABALA
> No...no...They would've used them
> before - if they had any...
>
> STEPAN
> Would they?
>
> DIETRICH
> You think that's it?
>
> STEPAN
> There's only one way to find out
> ...We'll have to spring the trap!
>
> ZABALA
> Wh-who...?

Stepan looks at him with contempt.

> STEPAN
> We'll draw lots...We'll all have
> an equal chance.
>
> ZABALA
> Wait...wait a moment...There must
> be something else...

His eyes dart around nervously; suddenly he gets an
idea.

> ZABALA
> Yes...I've got it...We don't have
> to endanger ourselves...Look...See
> that crevice?  In the rock wall?  It's
> only about ten feet from the trap...

(CONT)

450.  CONTINUED

> STEPAN
> What about it?

> ZABALA
> Don't you see?  A man could
> hide in there - safely.  And
> spring the trap with a long
> stick!

> STEPAN
> An excellent idea, Zabala.
> Do it!

> ZABALA
> (Taken aback)
> M..me?!...

> STEPAN
> You!  Get on with it!

451.  C.U.  ZABALA

He looks trapped...

                                    DISSOLVE

452.  EXT. DAY.  JUNGLE CLEARING.  CLOSE SHOT  DOCUMENT CASE

It is lying in the grass:  the grass rope can be seen
running off through the stalks and weeds...

Camera pans up to a MED. WIDE SHOT of the rock wall
and the crevice; Zabala - fearfully hugging the wall
- is warily making his way towards the safety of the
crevice; he carries a long stick in his hands; he
isn't taking his eyes off the fateful document case.

453.  TWO SHOT.  STEPAN AND DIETRICH.  ANOTHER PART OF THE
CLEARING

The two men are lying prostrate on the ground; Stepan
is watching through his binoculars.

> STEPAN
> He's almost there...

454.  MED. SHOT.  ZABALA

He is nearing the crevice; he looks extremely  nervous;
...finally he reaches the recessed nook, but he cannot
squeeze himself into it; a thick, dead branch blocks
his way.

455.   CLOSER ANGLE

Impatiently Zabala forces the dead branch aside; it
gives way with a creaking noise, as Zabala squeezes
himself into the narrow crevice...Suddenly there is a
gathering rubling sound from above...Zabala looks up...

456.   CLOSE SHOT.   TOP OF CREVICE

Shoving the dead branch aside has released a carefully
placed lever holding a huge rock in precarious balance
at the top of the crevice, ten - fifteen feet above
Zabala...The rock starts to tumble down...

457.   SPECIAL SHOT.  ZABALA.  P.O.V.  FALLING ROCK

Zabala is looking up; he is caught in the confining
crevice; his face mirrors unspeakable terror; his
mouth is open in a hoarse scream - as the heavy rock
crashes down upon him to - black!...

The trap is sprung!

458.   WIDE ANGLE.   THE CLEARING

Stepan and Dietrich are racing for the crevice; Zabala
is buried under the huge rock; a small avalanche of
stones and earth is following it down, making the job
complete; Stepan and Dietrich reach the spot.

459.   MED. TWO SHOT

There is nothing they can do; all that can be seen
of Zabala is one big, black boot sticking out from
the rubble.

                    STEPAN
        He was a coward...and a fool...

                    DIETRICH
                    (Awed)
        The very steps he took to be safe
        - killed him!

460.   ANOTHER ANGLE

Angrily Stepan strides to the document case; he snatches
up the loose decoy grass rope and hurls it away; then -
with shaking hands - he picks up the document case...

461.   CLOSE SHOT.  STEPAN

He rips open the case and tears out the contents; there
is one piece of paper - and a handful of large, folded
leaves!  Furiously Stepan crumbles the leaves in his

                              (CONT.)

461. CONTINUED

hand; he looks towards the jungle - literally shaking
with rage and frustration...

DISSOLVE

462. EXT. DUSK. L.S. TROPICAL BEACH

The jungle comes all the way down to the beach; there
is a stretch of rocky coast line to be seen. In the
distance three figures can be seen, stumbling out of
the jungle and making their way down to the water...

463. CLOSER ANGLE

It is Steve, Nita and Coman; their clothes are torn;
they are exhausted, bedraggled and nearly hopeless
as they stagger along the sandy beach to the edge of
the surf; Steve is supporting Coman, who is ill with
the burning infection in his arm. When the three
fugitives reach the water they walk at a right angle
to their trail leading unmistkably from the jungle
to the sea;  the gentle surf waves obliterate their
footprints as they slowly make their way towards a
rocky outcropping reaching from the jungle almost
to the water...

464. CLOSE THREE SHOT. TRAVEL SHOT. - TRUCKING

The three weary and battered fugitives stumble along
in the surf...Coman almost falls; Nita helps Steve
support him.

                    NITA
         We - can't...much longer...

                    STEVE
         It'll soon be dark.

                    NITA
         They can follow our trail - right to
         the water...

                    STEVE
         They won't know which way we've gon...
         the waves are washing our tracks away...

                    NITA
         Maybe we can find some place to hide
         - in the rocks...

465. MED. WIDE SHOT

The three fugitives are making their way towards the
rocks.

466. EXT. DUSK. MED. SHOT. ROCK OUTCROPPING.  CAVE MOUTH

The narrow opening to a small cave can be seen in the
rocky cliff;  it faces the beach; Nita comes climbing
into view; she sees the cave opening; she scrambles
over to it; looks in, and turns.

                    NITA
              (Calling softly)
        Steve!  Up here!...

Steve, supporting Coman, appears; Nita goes to help him.

267. CLOSER ANGLE

Nita helps Steve with Coman; Camera pans them to the
cave mouth, during:

                    NITA
        There's a cave over there...

                    STEVE
        Good...We'll stay there tonight...

They have reached the cave and start to enter it.

468. INT. CAVE. MED. WIDE SHOT

The entrance to the cave is narrow and twisted so that
there is no straight sight line into the interior, and
only one person at a time can enter or leave.  Behind
the entrance the cave is fairly large; Its floor is
soft sand; it is probably an old tidal cavern; there
is no other way in or out of the cave, but high above
a narrow rift in the roof lets in a pale shaft of light.
Steve, Coman and Nita enter the cave; they help Coman
to lie down; he is flushed and feverish...Steve and
Nita look around, then they sit down together - deeply
tired.  Camera dollies in to a CLOSE TWO SHOT.

                    STEVE
        Tomorrow...Tomorrow we'll look for
        a village...

                    NITA
        Tomorrow...What will happen tomorrow...?

Steve draws the girl over to him.

                              (CONT.)

                    STEVE
          There'll be a lot of tomorrows,
          Nita...I don't know what I'll do
          with them...I only know I want
          you to be a part of them...

Nita looks at him with her large, expressive eyes.

                    NITA
                  (Softly)
          With all my heart - I wish to be.

Steve takes her to him and kisses her; then holds her
close in his arms - her face hidden on his shoulder...

                    STEVE
          We've come this far...You'll see...
          We'll be alright...All of us...Nita
          ...Nita?...

The girl does not answer.

469.  WIDER ANGLE

Gently Steve lifts Nita from his shoulder; she is fast
asleep; with a little smile he lowers her to the soft
sand; then he bends over her and kisses both her eyes;
even in her sleep Nita smiles a little happy smile;
finally Steve lies down close beside the girl...

Camera pans off them to a CLOSE SHOT of COMAN; he, too,
is asleep - but he is uneasy and fitful...

                                        DISSOLVE

470.  INT. CAVE.  CLOSE SHOT.  STEVE

He is asleep; beside him sleeps Nita...Suddenly there
is a groan and a hoarse cry; Steve sits up with a
start to a C.U. - instantly awake.

471.  MED. SHOT

Nita, too, wakes up; Coman is tossing on the sand; it
is he who cried out; he is feverish, semi-delirious;
Steve and Nita hurry over to him.

472.  THREE SHOT

Steve quiets Coman; he relaxes.

                    NITA
          What is it?

                                        (CONT.)

472.   CONTINUED

                        STEVE
               The infection...It's beginning
               to spread...

Coman is mumbling feverishly.

                        COMAN
                    (With great urgency)
               Mintaka...Kimu...run...run...
               Kimu...

                        STEVE
               What's he talking about?

                        NITA
               Mintaka; Kimu...His wife - and
               his youngest boy...He had to leave
               them in the village...

                        COMAN
               Eneepe...my son...I join you...

Steve looks at Coman with compasionate understanding;
he rips a peice of cloth from his torn shirt.

                        STEVE
               Here...Go down to the water...wet this...

Nita takes the cloth and goes to the cave entrance;
Camera pans her over; she starts to leave.

473.   EXT. NIGHT.  MED. CLOSE SHOT.  CAVE MOUTH

Nita appears; she begins to get out of the cave - when
suddenly she stops and looks horrified...Camera whip-
pans to a REVERSE ANGLE L.S. DOWN THE BEACH, CAVE P.O.V.
At the spot on the beach where the three fugitives
entered the surf, a small fire burns brightly; two
figures can be made out sitting nearby.

474.   CLOSE SHOT.  CAVE MOUTH

Quickly Nita withdraws into the cave.

475.   INT. CAVE  MED. SHOT

Nita comes back into the cave.

                        NITA
                    (Frightened)
               They're here, Steve!  Right on the beach.'

Quickly Steve runs for the entrance; Nita follows him.

476. EXT. NIGHT.  CLOSE SHOT.  CAVE MOUTH

Steve and Nita appear, cautiously looking down the
beach.

477. L.S.  BEACH.  CAVE P.O.V.

The fire is burning brightly; the two men are there;
it is Stepan and Dietrich; one of them is throwing
more logs on the fire; the other is cleaning his
rifle; it gleams evilly in the light from the dancing
flames...

478. TWO SHOT.  STEVE AND NITA

                    STEVE
                 (Whispering)
          Only a couple of hundred yards
          away...

There is a sudden, faint hoarse cry from the cave;
quickly Steve and Nita duck back in.

479. INT. CAVE.  MED. SHOT

Steve and Nita hurry to Coman; he is groaning in
feverish delirium; Steve manages to quiet him down.

                    NITA
          They'll hear  him!

                    STEVE
          I know...If he screams - or calls
          out...Sound travels fast at night...

                    NITA
          What can we do?

Steve quickly walks around and examines the cave again,
minutely; there is absolutely no other exit; he returns
to Nita and Coman.

                    STEVE
          There's no other way out of here...

Camera dollies in to a CLOSE THREE SHOT.  Steve lifts
up Coman's injured arm; the make-shift bandage is
tattered and dirty.

                    STEVE
          There's only one thing we can do
          ...I'll have to lance the infection
          ...release the pressure...And hope
          his fever will go down...

                              (CONT.)

479.    CONTINUED

Nita looks at Steve, wide-eyed.

                    NITA
          But - the pain...He will scream...

                    STEVE
                  (Grimly)
          If he does...We've had it!

Coman groans again; he starts to cry out wildly; Steve
clamps his hand over his mouth until he subsides.

                    STEVE
          He'll get worse...We'll have to
          do it...You have to help, Nita.

The girl nods; Steve hands her his little knife.

                    STEVE
          Clean this in the sand - sharpen
          it on a rock as best you can...
          Then make a fresh bandage...

Nita carries out his instructions, during:  Steve brings
Coman out of his feverish sleep; the Indian sits up;
slowly he becomes rational; Steve tries to hold his
attention; Camera dollies in to a CLOSE TWO SHOT.

                    STEVE
                  (Urgently)
          Coman!  Listen to me.  Be very
          quiet.  Stepan is right outside.

Coman nods weakly.

                    STEVE
          You are very sick, Coman...The
          infection in your wound is making
          you sick.  You understand?

Again Coman nods.

                    STEVE
          I can help you.  I must cut the
          wound...Clean it out.  It will
          hurt...Much pain...And you must
          not cry out!  You understand?  Not
          a sound...

Coman looks at Steve earnestly; he nods.

                              (CONT.)

479.  CONTINUED

                         STEVE
               I'll have to cauterize the incision
               ...Burn it, Coman...you understand?
               Can you do it?

Slowly Coman's lips start to work...

                         COMAN
               You are my friend.  Evil spirits
               are in me.  You say cut them out!
               You say burn them!  I trust you.
               You do!

480.  ANOTHER CLOSE SHOT

Nita has finished her task; she hands Steve the knife,
and places the new bandage on the rock beside him.

                         STEVE
               Take the bandage off...

Nita does, while Steve takes out his handkerchief and
his cigarette lighter; he opens the lighter and pours
most of the fluid into a little hollow in the rock;
Then he makes a tourniquet on Coman's arm with his
handkerchief; Steve looks at Coman earnestly.

                         STEVE
               I'm ready, Coman.

                         COMAN
               You do!

Steve takes out his wallet; he holds it out to Coman.

                         STEVE
               Lie back, Coman...Bite on this...
               Bite hard!

Coman lies back; Steve places the wallet between his
teeth.

481.  CLOSE SHOT.  STEVE

He looks taut and grim; he picks up the knife; he
takes a deep breath...

482.  C.U.  NITA

She is watching him wide-eyed, but calm.

                                        (CONT.)

483.  CLOST TWO SHOT.  STEVE AND NITA

                        STEVE
                Hold his arm.

Nita does; Steve bends over it...He makes the incision...

484.  C.U.  COMAN

His eyes open wide with shock and pain; the sweat glis-
tens wetly on his forehead; the muscles of his jaw
cord as he bites down on the wallet...but he utters
not a sound.

485.  TWO SHOT.  STEVE AND NITA

Steve is working quickly, cleaning the absessed wound;
Nita looks drawn and shaken.

                        STEVE
                Light the fluid.

Nita lights the lighter fluid; a good-sized flame licks
up from the little hollow in the rock; Steve holds the
knife in the flame...

486.  CLOSE SHOT.  THE KNIFE

Slowly it glows red hot...

487.  CLOSE SHOT.  STEVE

He removes the knife from the flame; he looks down at
Coman.

                        STEVE
                      (Tensely)
                Once more, Coman...

488.  C.U.  COMAN

He looks at Steve with burning eyes; suddenly he winces
sharply and bites on the wallet with all his might; his
eyes strain as if to leave their sockets; there is a
faint hissing sound to be heard...

489.  C.U.  COMAN'S FREE HAND

It claws convulsively at the sand.

490.  THREE SHOT.

Steve removes the knife from the wound; he looks at

                                        (CONT.)

490. CONTINUED

Coman; Nita removes the wallet.

                    STEVE
          You are brave, <u>Sagala Coman</u> - Chief
          of the Cunas!

Coman grins broadly.

                    COMAN
          You fix.  Evil spirits go now!...

In utter exhaustion his head rolls over - and he is
asleep, even as Nita starts to bandage his arm...

                              DISSOLVE

491. EXT. SUNRISE.  L.S.  BEACH.  P.O.V.  ROCKS

The sun is just rising over the beautiful, peaceful
looking tropical beach; a couple of hundred yards away
Stepan and Dietrich are getting ready to take up the
pursuit...Camera pans to a CLOSE SHOT.  CAVE MOUTH:
Steve can be seen crouching there, watching the two
men tensely...Quietly Nita joins him.

492. CLOSE TWO SHOT.  STEVE AND NITA

                    STEVE
                 (Whispering)
          They're just about to start out...
          There're only two of them!

                    NITA
               (Softly; as if praying)
          Oh, please!  Let them go the other
          way!

They watch intently.

493. L.S.  BEACH.  CAVE P.O.V.

Stepan and Dietrich - guns in hand - are trying to
decide which way to go; they examine the trail made
by the fugitives in the sand from the jungle to the
surf; they look to the right and to the left...

494. CLOSE TWO SHOT.  NITA AND STEVE

                    STEVE
          How is Coman?

                              (CONT.)

494.	CONTINUED.

>                    NITA
>          Resting...The fever is gone...
>          Steve...What do we do - if they
>          come this way...?

>                    STEVE
>          Hide in the cave - and pray!

They watch the beach.

495.	L.S.  BEACH.  P.O.V.  CAVE

Stepan and Dietrich are standing at the surf; Dietrich
points towards the cave.

496.	CLOSE TWO SHOT.  STEVE AND NITA

Steve looks grim; Nita very anxious, as they tensely
await the decision of the pursuers.

497.	L.S. BEACH.  P.O.V.  CAVE

Stepan and Dietrich seem undecided; finally they begin
to trot down the beach - away from the cave.

498.	TWO SHOT.  STEVE AND NITA

They both look immensely relieved.

>                    NITA
>          Steve!  They're going away!  They're
>          going the other way!

Suddenly there is a raucous shriek above their heads
- again and again...Steve and Nita look up in alarm.

499.	SHOT.  P.O.V.  STEVE AND NITA

They are looking up; in the air just above their heads,
as they lie hidden at the cave mouth, a seagull is
hovering; she shrieks abuse; scolding and flapping her
wings as she dive-bombs at them - again and again...

500.	TWO SHOT.  STEVE AND NITA

They are looking up at the seagull; they look stricken;
the dreadful racket from above continues.

>                    NITA
>          What's it doing?

>                              (CONT.)

500.     CONTINUED

                        STEVE
               Her nest must be up there...She's
               just discovered us...She's trying
               to protect it!

He quickly turns to look down the beach.

501.     L.S.  BEACH.  P.O.V.  CAVE

Stepan and Dietrich have stopped; they are both looking
towards the cave.

502.     MED. SHOT.  STEPAN AND DIETRICH

Stepan stands a little ahead of Dietrich; in the
distance the raucous shrieks of the angry seafull can
be heard; Stepan gets an ugly, triumphant look on his
face.

503.     REVERSE ANGLE.  ACROSS DIETRICH AND STEPAN IN F.G. TO
         ROCKS IN B.G.

Both men are looking towards the rocks; the gull can be
seen circling and dive-bombing in the B.G.  Stepan turns
with a cold grin to Dietrich.

                        STEPAN
               Don't the Americans have a particularly
               obnoxious cliche:  A little bird told me!..?
               Come on!

They start to run towards the rocks...

504.     INT. CAVE MED. SHOT.  FEATURING ENTRANCE

Steve and Nita are crouched on one side of the narrow,
twisted entrance; Coman - his fever gone - is on the
other; from outside the scolding of the seafull can be
heard; then it disappears in the distance; for a little
while there is no sound from outside...

505.     TWO SHOT.  STEVE AND NITA

They hardly dare breathe; Nita looks at Steve; he is
listening - hard...

506.     C.U.  COMAN

His face looks hard and dangerous.

                                        (CONT.)

507. MED. SHOT

The three traped fugitives are listening anxiously;
suddenly Stepan's voice reaches them from the outside.

     STEPAN (O.S.)
   You might as well come out, Mr.
   Carter...I know you are there.

Nita starts; she huddles closer to Steve; he cautions
her to be quiet; he is clutching his little knife in
his hand until the knuckles show white...

     STEPAN (O.S.)
   Come now...It's no use pretending
   you are not there...

508. EXT. DAY. MED. SHOT. CAVE MOUTH - OVERLAPPING

Stepan and Dietrich are waiting at the cave mouth -
rifles pointed at the narrow entrance.

     STEPAN
   ...Your trail leads up here...None
   leads away...And there doesn't seem
   to be another exit - does there? Come
   out...You won't be harmed!

Both rifles are pointed at the cave; from the opening
comes Steve's defiant answer:

     STEVE
   If you want us, Stepan...Come in
   and get us!

     STEPAN
    (Patronizingly)
   I don't think that will be necessary.
   We have all the time in the world -
   now.  We can wait!

509. INT. CAVE. MED. SHOT

Nita looks up at Steve with large, frightened eyes.

     NITA
   Steve?

     STEVE
    (Grimly)
   He's right, Nita...We can't hold
   out for long - without food and
   water...We're trapped!

Coman starts for the entrance.

       (CONT.)

509.    CONTINUED

                    COMAN
          I go out.  Fight!

Steve stops him.

                    STEVE
          No, Coman...Stepan can't shoot in
          here - but you wouldn't live a
          second, if you show your head outside!

510.    EXT. DAY.  MED. SHOT.  CAVE MOUTH

Stepan and Dietrich are waiting.

                    STEPAN
          Well, Mr. Carter?

There is no answer from the cave; Stepan shrugs - and
the two men settle down to wait it out...

                                        DISSOLVE

511.    EXT. DAY.  CAVE MOUTH.  CLOSE SHOT.  SMALL FIRE

A small driftwood fire is burning on the rocks; Camera
pulls out to a MED. SHOT: Dietrich is sitting with his
rifle on his knees watching the cave entrance; Stepan
is finishing a meal from the provision carried in the
knapsacks.

512.    INT. CAVE.  TWO SHOT.  STEVE AND NITA

They are sitting near the entrance, close together;
Nita looks lost in thought.

                    STEVE
          What are you thinking, Nita?

                    NITA
                  (Softly)
          I was thinking...When I was a little
          girl...How happy I was with my father
          ...He would tell me stories...Wonderful
          stories...I was thinking...I wanted to
          tell those stories - to my children...

Steve looks around the cave.

                    STEVE
                  (With bitter frustration)
          If only there was another way out...

                                        (CONT.)

512.  CONTINUED

                         NITA
                  (Softly; in Spanish)
            "There is always a thrid way out..."

                         STEVE
            What did you say?

                         NITA
            It is from a story my father used
            to tell me:  "There is always a
            third way out..." - It had a lesson
            - a moral - that if you have a problem,
            where you think you must do either one
            thing, or another...there is always a
            third way out...

                         STEVE
                  (Musingly)
            A third way out...

Suddenly he sits up with a start; eagerly he lo ks at
Nita.

                         STEVE
            A third way out! There is, Nita!
            Your father was right!

Nita looks at him with astonishment - and with renewed
hope; Camera pulls back to include Coman; Steve turns
to the Indian.

                         STEVE
            Coman.  Have you still got that
            little blowgun.

                         COMAN
            Have got.

He takes the little blowgun from his belt; he hands it
to Steve.

                         STEVE
            Good.

He takes the blowgun; Camera dollies in to a CLOSE SHOT,
BLOWGUN, during:

                         STEVE
            Now - listen carefully...

                              DISSOLVE

513.    EXT. DAY. MED. SHOT.  CAVE MOUTH

Stepan and Dietrich are guarding the narrow entrance
to the cave - waiting patiently for what they <u>know</u>
must be the outcome of their vigilance...Suddenly
Nita's excited voice can be heard from the cave:

                    NITA (O.S.)
          Look!  A passage!  We can get out
          this way!

And Steve's  quick:

                    STEVE (O.S.)
          Quiet!  They'll hear you!

Stepan and Dietrich sit up alertly; Stepan motions for
Dietrich to take another look above the cave in the
rocks; Dietrich hurries away; Stepan moves closer to
the cave mouth; he listens.

514.    CLOSE SHOT.  STEPAN

He is listening intently; there is not a sound to be
heard from the cave.

515.    WIDER ANGLE

Stepan scrambles away from the cave; he looks up
towards Dietrich on the top of the cave; Dietrich waves
to indicate that there is no other exit detectable;
Stepan goes to the cave mouth again; Camera moves in
to a CLOSER ANGLE; Stepan looks worried; Dietrich
joins him.

                    DIETRICH
          There is no other exit.

                    STEPAN
                    (Frowning)
          It's a trick.  They're trying to
          make us leave here...to look for
          them...or to make us go in after
          them...

                    DIETRICH
          Maybe they <u>did</u> get out...We'd have to
          get after them - quick...

                    STEPAN
          They're still in there...

                    DIETRICH
          Can you be sure?!

516.   M.C.U.   STEPAN

                    STEPAN
                   (Angrily)
            No!

He frowns in furious concentration.

517.   MED. SHOT

Stepan stands up; he starts to take off his jacket...

                    STEPAN
                   (Loudly)
            It won't work, Mr. Carter!   I
            know you can't get out of there...

Stepan takes a stick from the fire wood pile and wraps
his coat around one end of it.

                    STEPAN
            Carter!   I want to talk to you...
            I'm coming in!
Slowly he starts to push the rolled up jacket through
the cave entrance...

518.   M.C.U.   STEPAN

Cautiously he is pushing the stick into the entrance.

519.   M.C.U. DIETRICH

He is watching tensely; he holds his rifle ready.

520.   MED. SHOT

Stepan has pushed the stick all the way in; he waits -
nothing happens.

                    STEPAN
                   (Calling)
            Carter!

There is no response - no reaction...Angrily Stepan
yanks the coat back out.

                    DIETRICH
            They could have found a passage -
            to an exit further away...

                    STEPAN
                   (Glowering)
            I know they're in there!

521    C.U.  DIETRICH

He looks at Stepan with scepticism.

522.   TWO SHOT

                    STEPAN
           We must make certain...We can't
           take the chance...
                    (Resolutely)
           I'm going in!

Stepan picks up his jacket; this time he wraps it around
his left arm as protection atainst a knife thrust.

                    DIETRICH
           What are you doing?

                    STEPAN
           They have a knife...I'm taking no
           chances...Take off your belt.

Dietrich does, as Stepan checks his pistol, which he
takes from his belt holster; then he takes Dietrich's
belt and fastens it to his own; he gives the other
end to Dietrich.

                    STEPAN
           Hold on to this...If they grab me
           - pull me out...

Then - slowly, cautiously - pistol in hand - left arm
held out before him, Stepan starts to enter the narrow
cave entrance...

523.   INT. CAVE.  CLOSE SHOT.  CAVE ENTRANCE

Slowly Stepan's arm - with the wrapped-around jacket -
comes into view, cautiously followed by Stepan himself;
he stops - looks into the cave.

                    STEPAN
                    (Sharply)
           Dietrich!  In here!

Camera pulls back to a MED. SHOT as Stepan steps into
the cave, quickly followed by Dietrich; the two men
look grimly surprised.

                    DIETRICH
           Empty!

524. REVERSE ANGLE.  ACROSS STEPAN AND DIETRICH TO CAVE
     INTERIOR

     The two men stand looking into the cave interior; all
     of it can be seen; it is completely bare - and empty!
     Stepan takes a couple of steps forward...Suddenly a
     pair of strong hands shoot up out of the soft sand
     floor to grab Stepan's legs and send him sprawling on
     the ground; before Dietrich can come to his aid another
     pair of hands springing from the sandy ground finds his
     own legs - and he goes down...And from the soft, sandy
     floor Steve and Coman emerge from their shallow graves
     to do battle with Stepan and Dietrich!!...

525. THE FIGHT

     The fight will be routined; it is a vicious, furious
     struggle; Steve and Stepan are locked together; Steve
     has his little knife; Stepan his gun; Coman and Dietrich
     are fighting too, the little Indian finding fantastic
     strength in his hate and fury; Steve forces Stepan
     to drop the gun...

526. CLOSE SHOT.  SANDY FLOOR NEAR CAVE WALL

     The fantastic, distorted shadows of the violently
     fighting men are dancing grotesquely on the rocky
     wall; Nita sits up through the sand; from her mouth
     she removes the little piece of the blowgun, through
     which she has been breathing, lying in wait in her
     shallow, sandy grave just below the surface - just
     like Steve and Coman...Quickly Nita takes in the
     situation...

527. THE FIGHT

     Steve and Stepan are fighting savagely; near them the
     gun lies in the sand.

528. C.U. NITA

     She sees the gun.

529. CLOSE SHOT.  THE GUN

     It is lying in the sand near the fighting men.

530. MED. SHOT

     Nita manages to get hold of the gun; she stands up -
     and fires a shot into the ground...The noise is ear-
     splitting in the confinement of the cave...

530.  CONTINUED

The men stop fighting at once; Steve leaps to Nita's
side; she is pointing the pistol unwaveringly at
Stepan - the man who killed her father...

531.  CLOSE SHOT.  NITA

Her large eyes are burning; slowly her hand tightens
on the gun...

532.  CLOSE SHOT.  STEPAN

Over his arrogant face creeps a mask of fear...

533.  MED. SHOT

Steve reaches for the gun in Nita's hand.

                         STEVE
                       (Quietly)
              I'll take it from here, Nita...We
              need this one alive!

                                   DISSOLVE

534.  EXT. DAY. L.S.  GATE TO SMALL COASTAL EMERGENCY LANDING
      FIELD

The gate is a pretty crude affair; over it is a sign
reading:

EMERGENCY LANDING FIELD # 7

In the B.G. the windsock can be seen flying over the
cleared field; also several huts...

A strange little procession is nearing the gate:  First
comes Coman - triumphant and important as a peacock, with
a rifle slung over his back; then Stepan and Dietrich -
tied with their hands over a long pole resting on their
shoulders they waddle on; and finally Steve and Nita -
Steve armed with Stepan's rifle and pistol...

From the landing field village a swarm of curious
villagers - led by a host of squealing children - come
running to meet them; among them is a small group of
village dignitaries; they meet with Steve and Nita.

535.  CLOSER ANGLE

Steve exchanges greetings with the villagers.

536.  CLOSE GROUP SHOT.  STEVE, NITA AND TWO RO THREE VILLAGERS

                         STEVE
               (He indicates Stepan and Dietrich)
                These men must be taken to the
                United States Air Force...right
                away...Albrook Field...

The villagers nod wisely.

                         STEVE
                Do you have any way of making
                contact with the Canal Zone?

Again the villagers nod elaborately,

                        VILLAGER
                Airmen have radio in hut on
                field.  You send message.  They
                come get you in big plane.

                         STEVE
               Great!

537.  WIDER ANGLE

They all start through the gate...

                                   DISSOLVE

538.  EXT. DAY.  L.S.  ALBROOK FIELD, A.F.B., PANAMA CANAL
      ZONE, HQ CARIBBEAN COMMAND.  (STOCK)  ESTABLISHING SHOT

539.  EXT. DAY.  L.S.  AIR FIELD (STOCK)

      Several troop transport planes are standing on the
      field; paratroops in full combat gear are loading on
      the double...Overhead a flight of jets roar by.

540.  ANOTHER ANGLE  (STOCK)

      A large transport plane is being loaded with field gun
      and jeep.

541.  VARIOUS SHOTS.  (STOCK)

      Different appropriate shots of planes being armed, etc...

542.  L.S.  TROOP TRANSPORT PLANES.  (STOCK)

      The paratroops have almost finished loading.

543.    EXT. DAY.  MED. SHOT.   AREA NEAR AIR FIELD

Duncan, Col. Bankes and Steve are standing together
watching the activity on the field.  Duncan has a locked
briefcase under his arm; in the B.G. can be heard the
sounds of airplane motors being started and reved up.

                    DUNCAN
          The C.I.A. owes you a great debt
          of gratitude, Mr. Carter.

                    BANKES
          We all do...
             (He indicates the field)
          It won't be long now, before Stepan's
          threat no longer exists!

                    STEVE
          I wish Grant and Warnecke could
          have been here...

                    BANKES
          Forget you ever knew them!

                    STEVE
             (Gravely)
          They were not the kind of men
          you forget!

                    BANKES
          Of course not...But at the risk
          of repeating myself, I want to
          impress upon you that everything
          that has happened is classified
          'top secret'...!

                    STEVE
             (With a little smile)
          I understand.

                    DUNCAN
          My plane is about ready to take off
          ...I'll have to have these documents
          in Washington by tonight...You're sure
          you won't come along?

                    STEVE
          I'm not quite ready to leave yet...

Duncan takes his hand.

                              (CONT.)

543.  CONTINUED

                              DUNCAN
              Thank you again, Mr. Carter...
              And I hope your - personal problems
              - will work out for the very best...

                              STEVE
                      (With a broad grin)
              They already have!

544.  EXT. DAY. MED. SHOT.  AREA NEAR GATUN DAM, LOCKS AND
      LAKE

      Nita is standing in the F.G.; she is looking out over
      a breathtaking, panoramic view of the Gatun Dam and
      Locks, and the big Gatun Lake; Steve comes up to her.

545.  TWO SHOT

      Nita looks out over the view.

                              NITA
              It's a beautiful spot...

                              STEVE
              That it is...And it'll be here to
              enjoy for a long time to come!

                              NITA
              Did you see Coman?

                              STEVE
              Certainly did...He was bursting with
              pride - going with the Task Force
              as Chief Interpreter!

                              NITA
              I wonder if we'll ever see him again...

                              STEVE
              We will.  He insisted we spend our
              honeymoon in his village!  With him
              and his family...

      There is the gathering noise of a large flight of planes
      passing overhead; Steve and Nita look up.

546.  SHOT

      Across the sky a flight of troop transport planes are
      winging their way towards the jungle; high above them
      several jets paint their delicate, white exhaust
      patterns across the clear, blue expanse...

547.   TWO SHOT.  STEVE AND NITA

They look at each other.

                    STEVE
          Well, darling...Can you think of
          any reasons why we shouldn't start
          on our tomorrows?!

Nita smiles happily and melts into Steve's arms.

548.   L.S. ACROSS STEVE AND NITA TO GATUN DAM, LOCKS AND LAKE

Arms around each other the two young people look out
over the grandeur of the scene...

FADE OUT

                    T H E   E N D

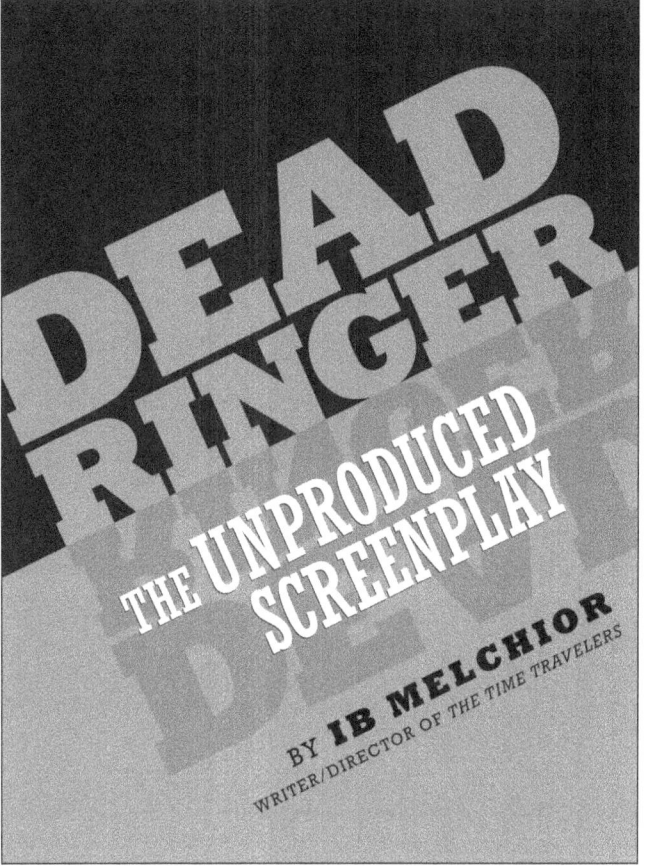
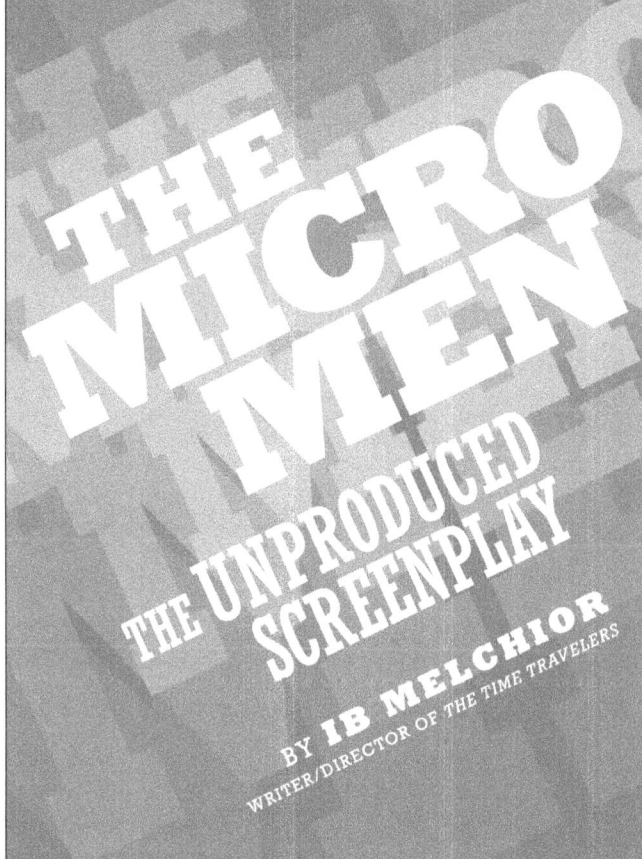

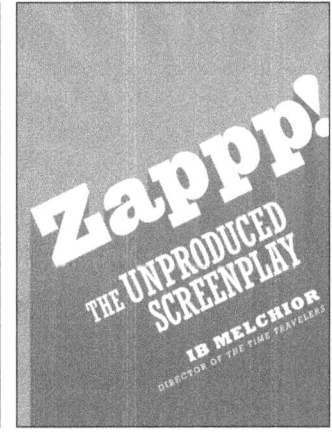

www.ingramcontent.com/pod-product-compliance
Lightning Source LLC
Chambersburg PA
CBHW080910020726
47502CB00008B/2411